Lincolnshire

COUNTY COUNCIL

COMMUNITIES, CULTURAL SERVICES
and ADULT EDUCATION
**This book should be returned on or before
the last date shown below.**

To renew or order library books please telephone 01522 782010
or visit www.lincolnshire.gov.uk
You will require a Personal Identification Number.
Ask any member of staff for this.

99 (LIBS): RS/L5/19

VIRGIN FOR THE BILLIONAIRE'S TAKING

VIRGIN FOR THE BILLIONAIRE'S TAKING

BY

PENNY JORDAN

MILLS & BOON®

Pure reading pleasure™

First published in Great Britain 2008
Large Print edition 2009
Harlequin Mills & Boon Limited,
Eton House, 18-24 Paradise Road,
Richmond, Surrey TW9 1SR

© Penny Jordan 2008

ISBN: 978 0 263 20562 6

Set in Times Roman 16¾ on 19¾ pt.
16-0209-51127

Printed and bound in Great Britain
by CPI Antony Rowe, Chippenham, Wiltshire

To my editor, for her patience

CHAPTER ONE

'EXCUSE me.'

Keira had been so focused on watching the bustle of guests in the ancient palace courtyard, where two of her closest friends had just married, that she hadn't realised that she was blocking the pathway to the garden. She had intended to make her way to one of the pavilions put up for the wedding celebrations, but had become distracted by the magical, intoxicating atmosphere of it all.

The male voice was authoritative and deep—velvet-rough, Keira decided, as though the nap of the fabric had been brushed to reveal the strength that lay beneath the silky surface. Just hearing it made her feel as though that same fabric had brushed against her own skin, and the sensual effect on her sent small electric shocks of awareness darting through her. His accent was recognisably English public school, and university honed: the accent of a man who took both position and wealth for granted as his right of birth. The accent of privilege, power and pride.

Would her accent give away as much about her? Would he sense the Northern accent she had learned to conceal beneath the tones she knew worked best for her in her business as an interior designer?

She turned towards him, her lips framing an apology for the fact that she had been so intent on watching what was going on that she had inadvertently blocked his way along the narrow path that led from the courtyard to the gardens. Her eyes widened as she realised she was looking at the most sexually compelling and dangerous man she had ever seen.

As though her whole body and all her senses had been hard-wired for this moment, every nerve-ending she possessed was reacting to him with a silent but violent intensity. It was like being physically attacked by her own body—like being mugged and having the protection of her normal caution stolen from her. She was frozen and wide-eyed, as aware of the dangerous nature of his impact on her as if she had been standing in front of an oncoming train.

The power of his sexuality slammed into her, leaving her unable to defend herself from it.

Jay didn't know why he was wasting his time standing here letting the woman stare at him in the way that she was, blatant in her awareness of him.

Admittedly she was beautiful. But she wasn't the only European guest attending the wedding, though with her looks and figure she would have stood out no matter where she was. Tall and elegant, she had a refined air about her whilst the lush curves of her body and the soft fullness of her mouth said clearly that hers was the kind of sensual nature he most enjoyed in a woman.

In bed she would display a sensuality that came straight from the most erotic pages of the *Kama Sutra,* enticing any man who became her lover into pleasuring her until she cried out against the intensity of that pleasure. He could see her now, her dark hair spread out against the pillows, her eyes luminous with arousal, the lips of her sex curving softly and moistly, waiting to open to his touch like the petals of a lily open to the heat of the sun, exposing the pulsing heart of their being, giving that most intimate part of themselves up to the sun's heat, spreading their petals in open appeal for its possession, the scent of their longing filling the air.

The sudden intensity of the sharp surge of desire hardening his body caught him off guard, causing him to shift his weight from one foot to the other.

At thirty-four he was more than old enough to be able to control his physical reactions to a desirable woman, and yet somehow this woman had him reacting to her so fast that he had been caught by the wayward direction of his own thoughts—and his desire for her.

She hadn't made any attempt to don the costume that the female Indian guests were wearing so confidently and elegantly, as some European women did when attending Indian celebrations. But none of those things would normally have been enough to counteract his belief that she was covertly suggesting to him that she was available, and thus by the law of probability was also available to any other man who might have chanced to cross her path. He waited for the desire she had aroused within him to be chilled by the distasteful idea he had deliberately conjured up, and frowned with the recognition that it had not done so.

He was even more stunned when he heard himself asking her, 'Bride or groom?'

'I'm sorry…'

'I was asking which side of the wedding party you belong to,' he told her.

His choice of the word 'belong' stung her pride and her mind with the familiar pain of knowing that there was no one in this world to whom she 'belonged', but it was somehow over-written by the intoxicating fact that his question suggested that he wanted to prolong his contact with her.

He was undeniably handsome. Tension bit into her, as though some instinct deep inside her had pressed a warning button, but to her shock her senses were refusing to listen to it. How old was she? Certainly too old to stare in open awe at a man, no matter how good-looking he was. And yet, like a child hooked on the adrenalin kick of sugar, despite knowing that it wasn't good for her, she just couldn't stop looking at him.

He was wearing a light tan linen suit of the kind favoured by wealthy Italians, and everything about him breathed cosmopolitan upper-class privilege, education and wealth. His skin had the right kind of warm olive tint to it to carry off the suit, just as his body had the height and the muscles. Were his shoulders really that broad? It looked like it from the way he moved.

And yet, despite everything about him that proclaimed old money and social position, Keira could sense within him another darker side, a marauding, dangerous ruthlessness that clung to him so powerfully she could almost smell it.

She fought not to be drawn into the aura of magnetism that surrounded him. If anything was intoxicating her then surely it must be this most wonderful of wedding venues.

Originally a summer palace and hunting lodge owned by an ancient maharaja, it had been converted into a luxury five-star hotel. Formerly an island palace, it was now connected to the shore by a handsome avenue, but the impression created as one approached was that the palace and gardens floated on the serene waters of the lake that surrounded it.

If it wasn't the venue then perhaps it was the sensual scent of the lilies resting on the still water of the pools that was having such a dangerous effect on her senses? Whatever the cause, it was in her own interests to remember that she was supposed to be a rational adult.

Keira took a deep, calming breath and told him firmly, 'Both. I'm a friend of the bride and the groom.'

A swirl of activity refocused her attention on the wedding party. Late afternoon was giving way to early evening darkness, and preparations were almost finished for the evening reception. The small flickering flames of hundreds of glass-covered tea lights were scattered artfully around the large courtyard and floating in the pools and fountains, and the lights reflected in the lake beyond it giving it a magical aura of romance.

Richly embroidered pavilions in jewel colours were being erected as though by magic, their gold threadwork catching the light, and the branches of the trees in the gardens beyond the courtyard dripped strings of tiny fairy lights, illuminating the paths that led to individual guest suites in what was now one of India's most exclusive hotel and spa resorts.

Soon the newly married couple and their families would be changing for the evening, and she needed to go and do the same, she reminded herself, and yet she made no move to step aside, thereby ending their conversation and allowing him to walk away from her.

Perhaps it was something to do with the late-afternoon sun that was transforming the sky above them from deep turquoise to warm pink, or the languorous heat turning the air soft with a sensuality that was almost like a physical touch against her skin that was causing her heart to thud with heavy-laden beats. Or perhaps it was the effect the man standing so close to her was having on her.

Something inside her weakened and ached. It was India that was doing this to her. It had to be. She was beginning to panic now, caught off guard and out in the open with nowhere to run by the shockingness of her own vulnerability to instincts over which she had previously believed she had total control.

She needed desperately to think about something else. The wedding she was here to attend, for instance.

Shalini had used the magnificent venue for her wedding as the inspiration for her choice of traditional clothes. Tom had thrown himself into it, and had looked amazing in his red and gold turban, his gold silk *sherwani* suit and scarf embroidered to match Shalini's gold and red embroidered lehenga.

Keira would have wanted to attend Shalini and Tom's wedding wherever it had been held; they, along with Shalini's cousin Vikram, were her closest friends. And when Shalini had told her that she and Tom had decided to follow up their British civil marriage with a traditional Hindu ceremony here in Ralapur, nothing could have kept Keira away.

She had been longing to visit this ancient city state. It had captured her imagination immediately when she had first read about it. But Keira hadn't just come here for Shalini's wedding and to see the city. She had business here as well. She most certainly hadn't come looking for romance, she decided, before elaborating on her presence at the wedding.

'I was at university with Tom and Shalini,' she explained, before asking curiously, 'And you?'

It was typical of her type of woman that her voice should be low and husky, even if the slight vulnerable catch in it was a new twist on the world's oldest story. He had no intention of telling her anything personal about himself, or the fact that his elder brother was the new Maharaja.

'I have a connection with the bride's family,' he told her. It was after all the truth, since he owned the hotel. And a great deal more. He looked out across the lake. His mother had loved this place. It had become her retreat when she'd needed to escape from the presence of his father the

Maharaja and his avaricious courtesan, who had turned his head so much that he'd no longer cared about the feelings of his wife and his two sons.

Jay's mouth, full-lipped and sharply cut in a way that subtly underlined its sensuality, hardened at his thoughts. He had been eighteen, and just back from the English public school where both he and his brother had been educated. That winter the woman who had stolen away his father's affections with her openly sexual touches and her wet greedy mouth, painted with scarlet lipstick to match her nails, had first come to Ralapur. A 'modern' woman, she had called herself. A woman who had refused to live shackled by outdated moral rules, a woman who had looked at Jay's father, seen his position and his wealth, and had wanted him for herself. A greedy, amoral harlot of a woman who sold herself to men in return for their gifts. The opposite of his mother, who'd been gentle and obedient to her husband, and yet fierce in her protective love of her sons.

Jay and his elder brother, Rao, had shown their outrage by refusing to acknowledge the existence of the woman who had usurped their mother in her husband's heart.

'You must not blame your father,' she had told Jay. 'It is as though a spell has been cast on him, so that he is blind to everything and everyone but her.'

His father had been blind indeed not to see the woman for what she was, but he had refused to hear a word against her, and Rao and Jay had had to stand to one side and watch as their father humiliated their mother and himself with his obsession for her. The court had been filled with the courtiers' whispered gossip about her. She had boasted openly of her previous lovers, and had even threatened to leave their father if he did not give her the jewels and money she demanded.

Jay had burned with anger against his father, unable to understand how a man who had always prided himself on his moral stance, a man who was so proud of his family's reputation, quick to condemn others for their moral lapses, should behave in such a way.

In the end Jay had quarrelled so badly with his

father that he had had no option other than to leave home.

Both his mother and Rao had begged him not to go, but Jay had his own pride and so he had left, announcing that he no longer wished to be known as the second son of the Maharaja, and that from now on he would make his own way in the world. A foolish claim, perhaps, for a boy of only just eighteen

His father had laughed at him, and so had she— the slut who had ultimately been responsible for the death of his mother. Officially the cause of her death had been pneumonia, but Jay knew better. His gentle, beautiful mother had died of the wounds inflicted on her heart and her pride by a tramp who hadn't been fit to breathe the same air. He loathed the kind of woman his father's lover had been—greedy, sexually available to any man who had the price of her in his pocket.

He had been reluctant to return to Ralapur at first, when Rao had succeeded their father, but Rao had persisted, and out of love for his brother Jay had finally given in. Even now he wasn't sure if he had done the right thing.

The boy who had walked away from a life that held the status of being his father's second son into an uncertain future where he would have nothing but his own abilities had returned to the place of his birth a very wealthy man, who commanded respect not only in his own country but throughout Europe and North America as well. A billionaire property developer with such a sure eye for a successful venture that he was besieged by people wanting to go into business with him.

Now he was old enough to understand the sexual heat that had driven his father to forsake the high-born wife he had wed as a matter of state protocol and tradition for the courtesan who had courted and mastered his physical desire. Jay could to some extent exonerate his father, but he could never and would never forgive the harlot who had shamed their mother and stained the honour of their family name.

Keira watched his expression change and saw cold hauteur replacing the earlier heavy-lidded sexual interest that had darkened his eyes. What was he thinking? What was responsible for that look of arrogance and pride? Did he know how daunting it was? Did he care?

'You're here alone?' Jay cursed himself under his breath for having stepped into a trap he had known was there. But secretly he had wanted to— just as secretly he wanted *her,* this woman with her high cheekbones and her soft full lips, her golden eyes and her pale, almost translucent skin.

Why on earth should he want her? Women like her were ten a penny. She wasn't wearing any rings, which might not mean anything other than the fact that no one had ever given her a ring expensive enough for her to want to wear it. His last mistress had only accepted the end of their affair after a swift visit to Graff, the famous diamond house in London, where she had quickly pointed out to him the pink diamond she had obviously already picked out ahead of their visit there.

If he hadn't already been tired of her the fact that she had chosen such a gaudy stone would have killed his desire for her. Like all his lovers, she had been married. Married women were far easier and less expensive to leave when the affair was over, since they had husbands to answer to.

Jay had no desire to marry, though his status as the second son of the late Maharaja meant that it would be expected that he would make a dynastic marriage to someone deemed high-born enough to become his wife, their marriage negotiated by courtiers and lawyers. Jay had a deep-rooted aversion to allowing other people to arrange his life for him, aside from the fact that he had absolutely no interest in bedding a naïve, carefully protected 'suitable' girl, whose virginity would be traded as part of the deal in the negotiations for their marriage.

Such a marriage would be for life. The truth was that he was vehemently opposed to making a long-term commitment of any kind to any woman. No way was he going to be forced to part with any of the vast fortune he had built up through his own blood, sweat and tears to some conniving gold-digger who thought he would be stupid enough to commit to her in the heat of lust, and would expect a handsome 'separation' settlement from him once that lust had cooled and he wanted to get rid of her.

Keira hesitated, well aware of her own vulnerability. But it wasn't in her nature to lie, and even if it had been she suspected that Great-Aunt Ethel, the cold and embittered relative who had brought her up after her mother had died, would have beaten it out of her.

'Yes.' Somehow she managed to stop herself from saying those telltale words, *And you?* But she knew that they were there, spoken or not, and it made her realise how far she had already travelled along a road that she knew to be forbidden to her. If the great-aunt who had brought her up—reluctantly—after her mother's death were here now, she would make it very plain what she thought of her behaviour in talking to a strange man, giving him heaven alone knew what impression of herself, risking bringing shame and disgrace on her family, just like...

Keira's heart was thumping with all the driven intensity of the thud of war drums, menacing as they came ever closer, pouring the sound of threat and fear into the pounding hearts of their enemy. She wasn't going to be trapped by her own panic, though.

Perhaps she *had* looked at him for a split second too long, but that did not mean anything—not in this day and age, when a woman could look as boldly at a man as she chose. *A* man, maybe. But never *this* man. This man would see such a look as a challenge, an infringement upon his male right to be the hunter, and he would react powerfully to it, taking... Taking what? Taking her?

The unwanted direction of her own thoughts was so shocking that she immediately recoiled, fighting to push them away as she struggled to force herself to look at him without giving herself away.

Heavens, but he was good-looking—more than good-looking. He wore his blatantly male sexuality with the same careless ease with which he wore his hand-stitched suit. But she, of course, was immune to the message being subliminally relayed to her by the suit and his sexuality. Wasn't she?

Keira shivered. It was never a good idea to

challenge fate. She knew that. This was a man who positively oozed a raw sexuality that had the air around him thrumming with male hubris and testosterone—a man who, without her being able to do a single thing about it, had got under her carefully constructed guard and forced her body to acknowledge his effect on it.

He wanted her, Jay admitted reluctantly. He wanted her very badly.

Her full-length cream skirt, worn with a round-necked sleeved top, and the fine long cream silk scarf she was wearing certainly stood out amongst the jewel colours most of the other female guests were wearing, giving her an angelic air despite the darkness of her hair. She looked ethereal, and fragile, but there had been nothing ethereal about the look he had caught her giving him a few seconds ago: the look of a woman whose sensuality was aroused and clamouring for satisfaction.

The courtyard was almost empty now, the other guests having made their way to their rooms to change for the evening reception, and they were alone together. A small frisson of something that wasn't entirely a warning shivered over her skin.

This was getting ridiculous—and dangerous. She should have stepped out of his path the second he had asked her to do so, instead of… Instead of what? Standing here, watching him, greedily absorbing every detail of his vibrant maleness as though she was savouring some forbidden treat? What was she going to do with those stolen images? Take them to her bed and replay them inside her head whilst she…?

She had to get away from him, and from the effect he was having on her. Keira turned to leave, and then froze as he stretched out his arm to rest his hand on the illuminated trunk of a tree on the other side of the footpath, blocking her exit. His fingers were long and tapered, his nails clean and well shaped. She drew in a ragged breath of sun-warmed air, inhaling with it the scent of the evening—and of him. She might as well have inhaled a dangerous hallucinatory drug, she acknowledged as her gaze lifted compulsively to his face. His eyes weren't brown, but the cool slate-grey of northern seas. Her gaze was drifting downwards to his mouth, and Keira knew that no power on earth could have stopped her looking at it. His top lip was well cut and firm, whilst his bottom lip was sensually full and curved.

As unstoppable as a tsunami, a surge of sensation broke deep inside her. She took a step forward, and then one back, making a small sound that contained both her longing and her denial of it. But both the backward step and the denial came too late to cancel what had come before them.

She was in his arms, his fingers biting deep into the soft flesh of her own upper arms, and his mouth was hard and possessive on hers in a kiss of such intimacy that it tore down the trappings of civilisation.

Neither his kiss nor her own response to it could have been more intimate if he had stripped her naked—and she had wanted it, had completely offered herself to him, Keira recognised with a violent sense of shock. She could hardly stand up, hardly breathe, hardly think for the rush of physical hunger consuming her. It swept through her, obliterating everything that stood in its way, a violent storm of need that had her frantically sliding her hands beneath his jacket and then over his chest, trembling with her need to touch him.

His mouth was still on her own, both plundering and feeding the tight, hot ache of desire deep inside her. Panic pierced the hot sweetness of her own dangerous pleasure. She could not, she *must* not allow herself to feel like this. Horrified by her own behaviour, she forced her heavy-lidded eyes to open and focus on him. A shudder of denial gripped her body as she pulled herself out of his arms, and told him jerkily, 'I'm sorry. I don't do this kind of thing. I shouldn't have allowed that to happen.'

Now she *had* surprised him, Jay acknowledged. He had been about to accuse her of trying to lead him on and then withdrawing to get him more interested in her, and her almost stammered apology had startled him.

'But you wanted it too,' he challenged her softly.

Keira wanted desperately to lie, but ultimately couldn't.

'Yes,' she admitted. The pain of her own weakness and self-betrayal was too much for her to bear. It had to be the Indian air that was causing her to behave in such a reckless way, making her break every promise she had ever made to herself. It could not be the man watching her! *Must* not be him.

Panic clawed at her insides. No doubt he felt he had every right to be angry, every right to demand an explanation. But there wasn't one she could give him, so instead she turned on her heel, half running, half stumbling through the starry scented darkness.

Jay made no attempt to stop her. Initially he had been more concerned about his own unwanted physical response to her than in taking things further. It had only been when she had pulled back that he had felt that dangerous male surge of sexual anger at her denial. But then she had gone and totally disarmed him with her admission, her apology showing him a quirky vulnerability that right now was having an extraordinary effect on him. She intrigued him, excited him, piqued his interest in a way that challenged him mentally as well as sexually.

He had simply been walking through the palace gardens when he had first seen her. He had planned to spend the evening going over some important documents and making some phone calls, but now he was thinking about putting all of that on hold.

A woman who could admit that she was in the wrong in any way, and most especially in her sexual behaviour, was a very rare creature indeed in his experience. She was here alone, she had admitted that she wanted him, and he certainly wanted her. Jay's mouth curled in a totally male half-smile of anticipation.

Keira didn't stop to look over her shoulder to see if *he* was still watching her. Once she was inside her room with her door locked she leaned back against it, unable to move whilst cold shock and nausea filled her. She started to shiver. What on earth had she done? And, more importantly why had she done it?

How had she let that happen, after all these

years—years during which she had worked so assiduously to make sure that it did not? Why, when she had so easily resisted the sexual appeal of so many other men, had she behaved like that with this one? What was so special about him that had so easily broken through the wall she had built around her own sexuality, setting it free to make its demands heard?

Panic was clawing at her like a wild animal desperate to escape captivity. She couldn't allow her sexuality its voice. She couldn't allow it to exist, full-stop. She knew that. Her great-aunt had warned her often enough what was likely to happen to her—the degradation she would suffer, the shame she would bring on herself and her great-aunt. Even though Ethel had been dead for nearly a decade, Keira could still hear her voice as she told her what would happen to her if she followed in her mother's footsteps.

Keira had been twelve years old when her mother had died and her great-aunt had taken her in—or rather had been forced to take her in or face her neighbours finding out that she had abandoned her. She hadn't wanted her. She had made that plain.

'Your mother was a slut who brought disgrace on this family. Let me warn you that I'm going to make sure that you don't turn out the same, even if I have to beat it out of you,' she had told Keira when the social worker who had taken her to her great-aunt's house had left, adding, 'I'll have no cheap little tart living under *my* roof and bringing shame on *me*.'

Because she was her mother's daughter, all it would take was one step in the wrong direction, her great-aunt had told her, to lead her into a life of sin.

And so Keira had learned to keep a guard on her heart and her body. When boys at school had called her 'frigid' and 'iron knickers' she had thrilled with pride rather than been upset. Slowly and carefully she had created for herself a non-sexual world in which she felt safe—a world in which she could never become her mother's daughter.

That world had been hers for so long she had assumed it would always be that way, and yet

shockingly now, out of the blue, she had discovered what it felt like to want a man—and with
such depth that it had left her reeling. And still
wanting him. *No!* But the real answer was yes.

She went hot and then cold. She started to
tremble and to shiver. Her whole body ached
and pulsed with unfamiliar sensations and
needs. She felt as though her mind was on fire
with her own feverish imaginings, and her body
too. It was like being in the grip of some kind
of fever. Perhaps she was. Perhaps that was why
she had reacted as she had. Was there a fever that
could cause a person to desire someone like
this? Of course she knew that there wasn't. So
what exactly had happened to her? Why was her
body still aching with the aftershock of what it
had wanted and been denied? Where had it
come from, that deep physical need so diamet-
rically opposed to everything she had taught
herself to be? Was this how it had started for her
mother?

She shivered again, even more violently,
feeling sick with fear and despair.

CHAPTER TWO

SHE couldn't stay in her room, no matter how much she felt like doing so, Keira acknowledged tiredly. Someone would be sent to find her if she didn't appear at the evening reception.

She showered and changed quickly into her evening outfit, a full-length embroidered silver gown, simply cut and softly shaped without in any way clinging to her body.

Why had he done it? Why had he kissed her in the first place? What message had she inadvertently given him? What had he sensed in her?

Keira knew that question would torture her for a long time to come.

Reluctantly she left her room and headed out into the night-scented darkness, walking slowly along the pathway back through the gardens to the courtyard.

Dhol players had been hired to provide music to welcome the guests into the courtyard, magically transformed for the evening into a small city of jewel-coloured pavilions inside which buffet meals were set out.

Later there would be a disco and dancing. Would *he* be there? Stop it, she warned herself. If an attempt to subdue both her panic and her insidious fascination for a man she had already decided she had to forget she had even met, Keira tried to focus on something else.

When the wedding celebrations were over she would be meeting up with the two men responsible for financing a proposed new development of exclusive apartments in the new city that would house Ralapur's developing silicon valley. One of these men she knew well, and had worked with before, designing and furnishing the interiors of his apartments both in Mumbai and the UK, but the other she did not. It would be a huge step forward career-wise if she were to be appointed as the designer for this new complex, and one that would be very important to her—not just for the income, although with all the problems she had experienced with her business over the last few months she did need that too.

Keira frowned. The initial cause of those problems had been her refusal to sleep with a client who, out of spite, had then refused to pay Keira's bill, claiming that the work she had done for him had not been satisfactory.

With her good name at stake, as well as a sizeable amount of money, Keira had been advised to take him to court, but the costs involved had put her off. Unlike Bill Hartwell, she was not in a position to afford a potentially expensive legal battle. And of course there was no way she could prove that Bill Hartwell's malice sprang from the fact that she had refused his advances.

In her line of business it didn't do to attack the reputation of a client—a fact that had been reinforced to her when Sayeed had warned her that his partner was very strict about those who worked for him adhering to his own code, and had to Sayeed's certain knowledge terminated contracts with those who broke the rules he imposed.

'He's very shrewd, very arrogant, and very demanding. He has the highest standards for business conduct of anyone I know—a man whose word literally is his bond—and of course he is extremely wealthy. We're talking billion-aire status, and all of it earned by his own en-deavours—he's not inclined to trust anyone until they have proved themselves worthy of that trust.'

Sayeed had made him sound so formidable that Keira suspected she would have turned down the opportunity he offered if it hadn't been for the dire state of her current financial situation.

It was perhaps foolish of him to decide to position himself here in the shadows on the pathway where they had met earlier, Jay acknowledged, but he knew of old that women tended to relish such touches. And he certainly wanted her to relish his touch as much as he intended to relish touching her, he admitted, grimacing wryly at his own mental *double entendre*.

Where was she? The festivities would be starting soon, and he had planned to cajole her away before they did to somewhere rather more private. The courtyard was already filling with wedding guests, their voices and laughter almost drowning out the sound of the musicians. The smell of food spiced the evening air, and children ran giddily in and out of the groups of adults, giggling with excitement.

Keira had almost reached the point on the path where she had heard him saying that fateful 'excuse me' when she was hailed by Vikram, Shalini's cousin and the fourth member of their close-knit group of friends.

'Keira—there you are. I was just coming to look for you.'

She was swept off her feet and into a fierce hug.

'Vikram, put me down,' she protested.

'Not until you kiss me,' he told her, straight-faced.

Keira shook her head at him. Vikram was passionately in love with an eighteen-year-old cousin, and equally passionately determined not to allow both sets of hugely delighted parents to put pressure on her to marry him until she had a chance to complete her education. When Keira had first met him she had been eighteen to his twenty-one, a new student at university against his seniority as a third-year. Vikram had laid siege to her and done his best to coax her into his bed. She, of course, had refused, and instead of becoming lovers they had become friends. He still liked to tease her about her 'primness', as he called it.

'You'd better put me down before someone sees us and tells Mona,' Keira warned him teasingly.

'Mona loves you every bit as much as I do, and you know it.' Vikram laughed as he set her down on her feet.

Imprisoned in the shadows, and unable to move away without them seeing him, Jay saw the intimacy between them. Hearing Keira's warning words, immediately he stiffened. She had lied to him about being there alone—just as she had lied to him with her false air of vulnerability and her equally false hesitant apology. It was obvious to him exactly what her relationship was with the man who was holding her.

'I'd better go,' Vikram told Keira. 'I've been deputised to go and find Aunt Meena. Remember to save me a dance. Oh,' he added, reaching into his pocket for his wallet and then opening it and removing a thick bundle of notes, 'I almost forgot—here's the money I owe you.'

He had asked her earlier in the year if she could help him to redecorate the new apartment he had bought, and of course she had said yes, giving her time and advice free, and getting him discounts on furniture bought through her own suppliers. It had still left him with a substantial bill, which Keira had covered.

Thanking him, she tucked the money away in her handbag.

Vikram, Shalini and Tom were her best friends, but not even they knew everything about her. There were some things she hadn't been able to bear telling them for fear of seeing them turn away from her in disgust and losing their friendship.

She watched Vikram lope away from her down the path, and then turned to continue on her way to the courtyard, her eyes widening in shock and the colour coming and going in her face as she saw the familiar figure standing on the path in front of her, his arms folded across his chest.

'Oh, it's you,' she said inanely.

There was something different about him—and not just because he had changed his clothes and was now wearing a dark suit and a white shirt with discreet gold links in the cuffs that looked every bit as expensive as the heavy gold watch strapped to his wrist. He looked—he looked frighteningly angry, she recognized. And something more—something that warned her he was dangerous which, incomprehensibly, her body found exciting.

'You'll have to forgive if me I was rather dense earlier. When you said no, I didn't realise it was because you're here to do business and we hadn't negotiated terms. You should have been more direct with me.'

Keira was stunned—and horrified.

'By the looks of it you left your last customer a very happy man.'

'You don't understand—'

'Of course I understand. You're a woman who hires out her body for male pleasure.'

'No!'

'Yes.'

When had he taken hold of her? She had no awareness of having moved, but she must have done, because now they were standing in the shadows off the path, and he had manacled her wrists in a grip that hurt. It hurt all the more so because she was struggling against it, and all her frantic attempts to break free of his hold were doing was bringing her up against his body, so that she could feel its heat and smell its alien maleness.

'Let go of me,' she demanded

'Did you enjoy playing your little game? Well, for your information I wasn't in the least deceived. It was obvious just what you are.'

'No—'

'Yes.'

They were only a few yards from the courtyard,

but for all the attention either of them were paying to the proximity of the wedding guests they might as well have been isolated from the whole of the rest of the human race. The air surrounding them positively crackled with anger and sexual tension, to the extent that Keira wouldn't have been surprised if sparks hadn't suddenly started visibly illuminating the darkness.

Jay dragged her closer to him. He couldn't remember a time when he had ever felt this kind of male pride–induced anger. It consumed him, sweeping away his normal restraint. Seeing her being held in another man's arms and enjoying being held there had unleashed it, and now it was demanding appeasement. He lowered his head toward hers, seeking revenge for her insult to his pride.

The rush of sensation pounding through her veins wasn't just a mixture of anger and fear Keira knew that. But she still froze into rigid rejection when his mouth covered hers. Angrily he nipped at her lower lip, shocking the rigidity out of her body and replacing it with a primeval angry heat of her own that came out of nowhere, compelling her to respond to him with equal ferocity.

How could such blatant savagery be so erotic? How could she feel as though something inside her was breaking apart and consuming her? How could she be standing on her tiptoes to take as much of his punishing kiss as she could get?

He freed one of her wrists to slide his hand into her hair, his fingers splayed against her scalp to hold her head still as he punished her mouth with kisses of such sensual savagery that they were almost a form of torture. A torture she never wanted to end.

The raw sound of their increasingly laboured breath broke the calm silence of the gardens with a raw sexuality that demanded greater intimacy—and privacy.

Jay drew Keira deeper into the shadows, his mouth still on hers as his anger burned into desire. His hand was on her breast, shaping its full softness. He felt her shudder when he rubbed the pad of his thumb across her fabric-covered nipple, tight and hard, already outlined by the moonlight for his visual pleasure. He could feel his erection straining against his clothes. He took her hand and placed it against it.

Keira closed her eyes. This could not be happening. But it was. And, worse, she wanted desperately for it to go on happening—so desperately that she would rather have done anything than stop.

Not even the full spread of her fingers was enough to encompass the length of him, hard and pulsing with a driving demand that her own flesh ached to answer. His tongue probed between her lips, his fingers plucking rhythmically at her nipple, swollen and tight in its eagerness to entice him and be pleasured by him. If they hadn't been out here in the garden he could have removed her dress and pleasured it properly, with his mouth as well as his hands.

As though he had read her thoughts she felt him reach for the zip on her dress and slide it down. Instead of objecting, she shuddered with excited pleasure.

Jay felt her body's reaction to his touch, and a thin, cruel smile curled his mouth as he released hers from its possession. Not a true professional, then. If she was she would not have allowed her own desires to be so easily read. She was more of a greedy, highly-sexed woman, who had learned that men were willing to pay for her pleasure and their own sexual satisfaction.

Overhead in the courtyard fireworks started to explode, the noise shattering the highly charged sexual spell Keira was under and bringing her back to reality. As the first bright pink stars fell down to earth Keira pushed Jay away with a vehement, *'No!'*

What on earth was she doing?

Clumsy, but effective, Jay acknowledged. Get a man so wound up that he was prepared to do anything to get satisfaction and then demand a sweetener. It would be a new experience for him to pay a woman for sex—normally they ended up begging him for it, not the other way around.

Keira watched dazedly as Jay reached into his jacket pocket and removed his wallet. But it wasn't until he opened it to withdraw some crisp notes, demanding coldly, 'How much?' that she realised what he was doing.

Nausea clawed at her stomach, humiliation burning her like acid.

'No,' she repeated, stepping back from him so that he couldn't see how badly she was trembling, how dirty and ashamed she felt.

She was turning him down? How dared she— a woman he had already seen take money from one man tonight? Jay could barely contain his fury.

'I wasn't offering to pay for more,' he told her in a voice as soft as death. 'Having tested what's on offer, I find you aren't worth buying. I was simply offering to pay for what I'd already had. Here...'

As he stretched out his hand to push the money down the front of her dress Keira pushed his hand away and stepped back from him, telling him fiercely, 'I'm not for sale.'

'Liar.'

He had gone before she could say anything else, leaving her to struggle to re-zip her dress and then hurry to the nearest cloakroom to repair the damage to her face and hair before going to join the other wedding guests in the courtyard.

It was an effort for her to behave normally. She was still in shock—a double shock now, after the accusation he had flung at her. She felt more frightened and alone than she could ever remember feeling. Even as a young girl, when she had first realised exactly what her mother was.

'Your mam's a prostitute. She goes with men for money.'

She could still hear the sharp Northern tones of the boy who had cornered her in the school playground and chanted the words to her. She had been eight, and well aware that her home life was different from the lives of the other children at school—children whose mothers waited for them outside the school gates and pulled them away when they saw her, children who didn't go home to a mother who slept all day and 'worked' all night to pay for her drug habit.

Sometimes it seemed to Keira that she had

always known shame in one form or another, and that it had been her single true companion for all of her life, shadowing her and colouring her life—her future as well as her past.

CHAPTER THREE

JAY was a man who prided himself on his self-control. It was that control that ensured he would never repeat his father's folly in allowing his desire for an unworthy and avaricious woman to rule and humiliate him. Jay could allow himself to satisfy his physical desire, but he must always be the one to control it rather than the other way around. No woman had ever been allowed to intrude into his thoughts when he did not want her to, and yet now here he was, wasting his valuable mental energy thinking about a woman he despised. The mere fact that she was there in his thoughts, occupying space that rightly belonged to far more important matters, angered him far more than the unsatisfied ache of the desire she had left him with.

Why was he bothering to think about her?

She'd probably thought she was being extremely clever, that by offering and then withdrawing she would get far more from him than if she had simply gone to bed with him there and then, but Jay did not allow anyone to manipulate him to their own advantage—especially not the kind of woman who tried to play games with him. He had desired her, she had recognised that fact and responded to it, and then she had tried to make capital out of it. So far as he was concerned that meant game over.

Jay wasn't the kind of man who let his physical desires rule him, and it wasn't as though he wasn't used to women coming on to him. Coming on to him, yes. But then walking away from him having done so? He wasn't used to that, was he? It stung his pride—all the more so because of the type of woman she so obviously was. She was a fool if she thought he had been taken in by her puerile attempt to make him want her more by pretending that she didn't want him. And she was a fool because she had already previously admitted to him that she *did* want him. But she had still walked away from him. That knowledge rubbed against his pride as painfully as the sand of the nearby desert could rub against unprotected flesh.

Jay and his brother Rao had ridden their horses there as boys. He had a sudden longing for the freedom of the desert now, for its ability to strip a man down to his strengths and lay bare his weaknesses so that he was forced to overcome them to survive. The desert was hard taskmaster but a fair one. It taught a boy how to become a man and a man how to become a leader and a ruler. He had missed it in the years of his self-imposed exile, and one or the first things he had done on his return, following Rao's letter to him warning him of their father's imminent death, had been to have a horse saddled up so that the could ride free in the desert.

Rao would be a good and a wise ruler. Jay loved and admired his elder brother, and was grateful to him for the compassion he had shown in making sure that Jay had the opportunity to make his peace with their elderly father before his death.

The courtesan who had caused the original breach between them had long gone, having run off with her young lover and a trunk filled with not only the jewels her besotted lover had given her, but also some she had 'borrowed' from the royal vault and had never returned…

'I've set up an appointment for you with Jay. Unfortunately I can't stay with you, as I've got another meeting to go to, but he's cool about the idea of having you on board as our interior designer.'

While she was grateful to Sayeed for accompanying her to the meeting, Keira was also regretting the fact that she wasn't on her own and so able to study her surroundings more closely, she acknowledged as they walked together through the old city.

Somehow she hadn't expected the billionaire entrepreneur who was the driving force behind some of the most modern office structures currently going up around India to have his office in an ancient palace within the heart of Ralapur's old town.

'Jay doesn't make a big deal of it—as I've already said, he's fanatical about his privacy, and who he admits to his inner circle—but the truth is that his father was the old Maharaja, and until his brother marries Jay is his heir and next in line to the throne. The old Maharaja had been in poor health for a number of years before his death. He was very anti the modern world. Rao and Jay want to bring the benefits of modern life to the city and their people, but at the same time they are both dedicated to maintaining all those traditional things that makes Ralapur the very special place that it is. That is why all the new development will be outside the city.'

Sayeed was right in saying that Ralapur was a very special place, and Keira could well understand why the new Maharaja and his brother were determined not to see it spoiled. Her own artistic senses feasted on the array of ancient buildings. She couldn't make up her mind which form of architecture actually dominated the town. There was undoubtedly a strong Arab influence, but then according to legend one of Ralapur's first rulers had been a warrior

Arab prince. The Persian influence of the Mughal emperors could also be seen, as well as the tranquil calm of Hindu temples. She would have loved to stop to explore and enjoy the city at a more leisurely pace.

They had walked through the town from a large new car park outside the walls, where everyone was required to leave their vehicles because of the city's narrow, winding and frequently stepped streets. Now they had emerged from the cool shadows of one of those streets into a large square in front of the blindingly white alabaster-fronted royal palace. Two flights of white steps led up to it, divided by a half-landing on which stood two guards in gold and cream Mughal robes and turbans, their presence more for effect than anything else, Keira suspected.

Facing each other across the square, adjacent to the main palace, were two equally impressive but slightly smaller palaces, and it was towards one of these that Sayeed directed her.

'Jay has taken over the palace that was originally built for a sixteenth-century Maharaja, whilst the one opposite it was built at the same time for his widowed mother, who had been a famous stateswoman in her own right,' he said.

Sayeed spoke briefly to the imposing-looking 'guard' at the entrance before urging Keira up the flight of marble stairs and into a high square hallway that lay beyond them. She was feeling increasingly nervous by the minute. It had been bad enough when she had believed that her prospective client was an exacting and demanding billionaire, but now that she knew he was also a 'royal' her apprehension had increased.

He might be royal, but she was a highly qualified interior designer, who had trained with one of the most respected international firms, and whose own work was very highly thought of. She had very high standards and took pride in the excellence of her work, she reminded herself stoutly. She was a professional interior designer, yes. But she was also the daughter of a woman who had sold her body to men for money to feed her drug habit. Where did that place her on the scale of what was and what was not acceptable? Did she really need to ask herself that question? Of course she didn't. The burn of the shame she had known growing up because of her mother was still as raw now as it had been then.

It hadn't just been her great-aunt who had rammed home to her the message that her mother's lifestyle made Keira unacceptable and unwanted in more respectable people's social circles.

After her mother had died and her great-aunt had taken her in, Keira had had to change schools. In the early days at her new school another girl had befriended her, and within a few weeks they'd been on their way to becoming best friends. Keira, who had never had any real friends before, never mind a best friend, had been delirious with joy.

Until the day Anna had told her uncomfortably, 'My mother says that we can't be friends any more.'

By the end of the week the story of her mother had gone round the playground like measles, infecting everyone and most especially Keira herself. She'd been ostracised and excluded, forced to hang her head in shame and to endure the taunts of some of the other children.

Keira had known then that she must never allow people to know about her mother, because once they did they would not want to know her. She had made a vow to herself that she would not just walk away from her past at the first opportunity. She would build a wall between it and her that would separate her from it for ever.

Her chance to do just that had come when her great-aunt had died of a heart attack, leaving Keira at eighteen completely alone in the world, and with what had seemed to her at the time an enormous inheritance of £500,000.

She had bought herself elocution lessons so that she could hide her Northern accent, and with it her own shame, and the money had also helped her to train as an interior designer. It had bought her a tiny flat too, in what had then been an inexpensive part of London but which was now a very up-and-coming area.

As a child Keira had loved her mother. As she'd got older she had continued to love her, but her love had been mixed with anger. Now, as an adult, she still loved her—but that love was combined with pity and sadness, and a fierce determination not to repeat her mother's errors of judgement and weaknesses.

Keira never lied about her past. She simply didn't tell people everything about it, saying only that she had been orphaned young and brought up by an elderly great-aunt who had died just before she started university. It was, after all, the truth. Only she knew about the darker, more unpalatable and unacceptable parts of her past. A past that would certainly render her unacceptable to someone of such high status as a royal prince.

They were being guided to the main reception room—a huge, richly decorated room with columns and walls of gilded carvings designed to overwhelm and impress.

Don't think about the past, Keira urged herself. Look at the décor instead.

An Arabic-style fretted screen ran round an upper storey walkway, allowing those behind it to look down into the hallway without themselves being seen. It seemed to Keira that the very air of the room felt heavy with the weight of past secrecy and intrigue, of whispered promises and threats, and of royal favour and power courted and brokered behind closed doors.

This was a different world from the one she knew. She could feel its traditions and demands pressing down on her. Here within these walls a person would be judged by who their ancestors had been—not what they themselves were. Here within these walls she would most definitely have been judged as her mother's daughter, condemned and branded to follow in her footsteps by that judgement. Keira repressed a small shudder of apprehension as she followed Sayeed deeper into the room.

The scent of sandalwood filled the still air. High above them on the ceiling, mirrored mosaics caught the light from the narrow windows and redirected it so that it struck the gaze of those entering the room, momentarily blinding them and of course giving whoever might be standing behind the screens watching them, or indeed waiting for them in the room itself, a psychological advantage.

Sayeed gave their names to the man who appeared silent-footed and traditionally dressed, and then bowed to them and indicated that they were to follow him down a narrow passage behind the fretted screens. It led to a pair of double doors, which in turn opened into an elegant courtyard. He led them across and then in through another door and up a flight of stairs until they came to a pair of doors on which he knocked before opening.

A man speaking into a mobile phone was standing in front of a narrow grilled open window through which Keira could see and hear the street.

No, not *a* man, Keira recognised with a sickening downward plunge of her heart as he turned round towards them, but *the* man—the man for whom she had broken the most important rule in her life; the man she had kissed and touched and told without words but with a feverish intensity that had been quite plain that she desired him; the man from whom she had then run in her shame and her fear. The man who had shown her his contempt and his evaluation of her by offering her money in exchange for the kisses they shared.

If she could have done so Keira would have turned and run from him, from all the dark despair of her most private fears—fears which he had given fresh life both through her own desire for him and his treatment of her. But she couldn't. Sayeed was standing behind her.

The slate-grey gaze flicked over her and rested expressionlessly on her face. He had recognised her even if he wasn't showing it.

Sayeed stepped forward to shake the other man's hand, saying to him jovially, 'Jay. I've brought you Keira, just as I promised. She's desperate for you to give her this contract so that she can show you what she can do. I don't think you'll be disappointed by what she can offer.'

Keira squirmed inwardly over Sayeed's unfortunate choice of words and all that might be read into them by a cynical, sexually experienced man who had every reason to believe he already knew what she had to offer.

'I can't stay,' Sayeed was continuing. 'I've

got a meeting I have to attend, so I'm going to have to leave you to discuss things without me. However, as I've already told you, I've seen Keira's work, and she has my personal recommendation and endorsement.'

He had gone before she could stop him and tell him that she had changed her mind. That she wouldn't want this contract if it was the last one on earth.

Jay watched her. Unless she was a far better actress than he believed, she hadn't faked her shocked surprise at seeing him and realising who he was. So, a woman who hired herself out for sex? Or a professional woman who liked to let her hair down and play a game of sex tease with what she thought was the local talent? Or maybe a bit of both, depending on her mood? If so, perhaps she was more used to being paid off in expensive gifts rather than hard cash— although she hadn't looked unhappy to receive the bundle of notes he had seen her being given last night. She was dressed today for a business appointment—European-style, with a careful nod in the direction of Indian culture. He could see the faint beading of sweat on her upper lip—caused, he suspected, not so much by the heat as by her discomfort at seeing him again.

'You come highly recommended. Sayeed can't praise your skills enough.'

The taunt that lay beneath his words was barely veiled and intended to be recognised.

Keira could feel the slow painful burn of a feeling that was a mixture of shame and anger. That her own behaviour was the weapon she had handed him to use against her was the cause of her shame, and that he had not hesitated to use it the cause of her anger.

Well, she wasn't going to respond to his goading.

Jay frowned when she remained silent.

It irked him that he hadn't guessed who she might be, and it irritated him even more that she had brought with her into his office not just the scent of the perfume she was wearing but also the memory of his desire for her. And not only the memory, he realised as his body reacted to her against his will.

She wore her sexuality like she wore her scent, bringing it with her into his presence and forcing recognition of it on his senses whilst maintaining an air of detachment from it and from him.

He turned from her and strode the length of the room, trying to force down the ache that somehow managed to surface past his angry contempt.

He was pacing his office floor in such a way that she could almost hear the pad of a hunting cat's sharp-clawed paws, along with the dangerous swish of its tail—as though her mere presence fed his hunger to destroy her, Keira thought sickly.

'Has Sayeed bedded you? Is that why he is so keen to secure this contract for you? Did he promise it to you in exchange for your sexual favours?'

'No. I don't go to bed with anyone to secure business. I don't need to,' Keira told him proudly. 'My work speaks for itself.'

'Yes, indeed. I saw that for *myself* last night.'

The blood surged and then retreated through her veins, causing her heart to thud erratically.

There was no mistaking the meaning behind his words.

'You must think what you wish. Plainly that is what you intend to do.'

'It isn't my wishes that govern the logic of my thinking process, rather it is the visual evidence of my own eyes. I saw the man you were with handing you money—and rather a substantial amount of money at that.'

Keira had to defend her professional reputation. She wasn't going to get the contract, so she had nothing to lose in defending herself, had she? She took a deep breath and spoke swiftly.

'And because of that you leapt to the conclusion that I am…that I…that my body is for sale? That isn't logic. It is supposition tainted with prejudice.'

She was daring to argue with him? Daring to defend the indefensible and accuse him of being prejudiced? Jay could feel his fury pressing against the cords of his self-control, threatening to break free.

'He gave you money. I saw that with my own eyes.'

'He is an old friend. He was paying me for the refurbishment of his flat. If you don't believe me you can ask him—and you can ask Shalini as well.'

'Shalini?'

'The bride. She and Vikram are cousins. The two of them and Tom, Shalini's new husband, and I were all at university together.'

Keira had no idea why she was telling him all this. What difference could it make now? She had lost the contract, and despite the fact that she desperately needed the money a part of her was relieved. There were some things that mattered more than money, and her own peace of mind was definitely one of them.

Jay frowned. Something told him that she was telling the truth. Not that he had any intention of demeaning himself by questioning others about her.

And besides, there were other issues at stake here. She had an impressive client list, the majority of whom were women. That had been one of the most important deciding factors in his original decision to take her on. India's growing middle class wanted new and more westernised homes, and it was predominantly the women who were making the decisions about which developer they bought from. The interior of any new property was a vitally important selling point, and Jay knew that he could not afford to make any mistakes in his choice of interior designer.

On paper, this woman ticked all the right boxes. She had connections with an elite of London based Indian families—no doubt through the friendships she had made at university. She had worked for them in London, and he was well aware of the praise she had been given for the way she blended the best of traditional Indian and modern Western styles to create uniquely stylish interiors that had delighted their owners. She had also worked in Mumbai; she was at home in both cultures and apparently well liked by the Indian matriarchs whose approval was so vitally important to her business and indirectly to his.

His long silence was unnerving her, Keira admitted inwardly. It flustered her into repeating, 'My work speaks for itself.'

'But perhaps your body language speaks more clearly? To my sex at least.'

His voice was as cool as steel and just as deadly. Keira could feel it piercing her pride, taking a shimmering bead of its life force as though it were a trophy. Now that he had savoured his pleasure in wounding her no doubt he would close in for the kill and tell her that he wasn't going to give her the contract.

She lifted her chin and told him proudly, 'I don't see the point in prolonging this conversation, since it's obvious that you don't have any intention of commissioning me to work for you as an interior designer.'

He certainly didn't *want* to do so, now that he knew who she was, Jay acknowledged. But there was the delicate matter of losing face— both for Sayeed and in a roundabout way for Jay himself.

Sayeed might be a very junior partner in their current venture, but he would be within his rights to question why Jay had rejected Keira, after allowing the negotiations to get this far. Sayeed would be personally insulted, and whilst Jay was too rich and too powerful to worry about that, his own moral scruples were such that bringing his own personal feelings into the business arena was something he just would not do without explaining. That would cause *him* to lose face.

The situation was non-negotiable—both practically and morally. He had no alternative but to go ahead and formalise the offer of a contract, as Sayeed would be expecting him to do.

'Not personally, no,' he agreed silkily. 'So if last night's little game of tease was meant to whet my appetite I'm afraid it failed. However, when it comes to the contract for the interior design work at my new development, I am prepared to accept Sayeed's recommendation that you are the right designer for the job. Of course if he is wrong...'

Keira was struggling to take in the triple whammy effect of his speech—first the direct attack on her personally, then the surprise offer of the contract, and finally the killer blow, warning her that Sayeed would be the one who would end up losing out if she failed to live up to his recommendation. She was trapped, and they both knew it. Whilst she might have been willing to risk turning her back on the commission and fees for the sake of her own pride, she was not prepared to risk injuring Sayeed's business reputation by doing so. And she suspected that the man in front of her watching her, so cynically, knew that.

'Very well,' she told him, drawing herself up to her full height of five feet nine—which, whilst tall, was well below his far more impressive six foot plus, leaving her in the ignominious position of having to tilt her head back to look up at him. 'But I want it understood that the relationship between us will be purely and only that of developer and interior designer. Absolutely nothing more.'

She was *daring* to warn him off?

Jay couldn't believe her gall. Well, two could play at that game.

'Are you sure that is all you want?' he mocked her.

Keira could feel her face burn.

'Yes,' she confirmed, tight-lipped.

'Liar,' Jay taunted. 'But it's all right, because I assure you that I have no intention of our relationship being anything other than strictly business. The truth is that if you want me you're going to have to come crawling on your knees and beg me. And even then...' His gaze flicked over her disparagingly. 'Well, let's just say I'm not a fan of used goods.'

If she could have walked out, Keira knew that she would have done so. But she couldn't. Not now. He had trapped her with his implied threat about his business relationship with Sayeed.

The door to the room suddenly opened inwards to admit Sayeed himself, who told them both cheerfully, 'My appointment was cancelled, so I came back. How's it going?'

It was Jay who answered, telling him smoothly, 'Since Miss Myers comes with your recommendation, Sayeed, I am prepared to offer her a contract. Whether or not she chooses to accept it is, of course, up to her.'

Keira gave him a burning look. He knew perfectly well that her choices were non-existent. He had arranged matters so that they would be.

'Of course she'll accept it.' Sayeed was beaming enthusiastically.

'So that's agreed, then. Keira is coming on board as our designer,' Jay said briskly. 'I'll get my PA to sort out the contracts, and the three of us can have dinner tonight to celebrate and discuss everything in more detail. You're staying at the Palace Lodge Hotel, Keira? I'll have a car sent to pick you up at eight o'clock.'

It was a fiasco. No—worse than that; it was a total nightmare, Keira decided grimly later in the day as she walked through the city, trying not to let despair over her situation prevent her from enjoying exploring the city's unique cultural history.

Keira couldn't remember how old she had been when she had first realised just what her mother was. But she could remember that she had been nine when her mother had told Keira that her father was a married man.

'Loved him, I did—and he said he loved me.

Mind you, they all say that when they want to get into your knickers. Not that he were me first—not by a long chalk. Had lads running after me from when I was fourteen, I did. That's been my problem, see, Keira. I always liked a good time too much. It's in me nature, you see, and it will be in yours too—see if it isn't. We just can't help ourselves, see. Come from a long line of women made that way, you and me have. Some lad will come along, and before you know where you are you'll be opening your legs for him.'

Keira still shuddered when she remembered those words. They had filled her with a fear that her great-aunt's unkindness had reinforced. Keira had decided long before she went to university that she would never allow herself to fall in love or commit to a man because of the risk of discovering she shared her mother's weakness in controlling her sexual appetite, along with her inability to choose the right man.

Her horror of sharing her mother's fate was burned into her heart.

After university Keira had moved to London

and found a job working for an upmarket interior design company at a very junior level.

Through Shalini and Vikram she'd been familiar with the ethnically diverse Brick Lane area of the city, and she had quickly fallen in love with the creative intensity it had to offer, putting what she'd learned from it into her own work and adapting it to her own personal style.

Soon word had begun to get around that she had a sympathetic understanding of Indian taste, and rich Indians had started to ask specifically if she could be part of the team working on their interiors.

With the encouragement of her boss, Keira had eventually struck out on her own, finding for herself a niche market that was fresh and vibrant and matched her own feelings about design and style.

She'd met Sayeed through Vikram, and had let him sweet-talk her into doing some room schemes for the rundown properties he was doing up as buy-to-lets. Sayeed had done well, and an uncle in India had taken him into his own property development business—which was how Sayeed had become involved with Jay.

Jay. The thought of him—or rather of His Highness Prince Jayesh of Ralapur—was enough to have her tensing her body against her own inner panic. How could she have let such a thing happen to her?

It should have been impossible for him to have aroused her as he had done. Not once before had Keira ever felt tempted to ignore the rules she had made for herself.

Yes, she had kissed boys at university—she hadn't wanted to be thought odd or weird after all—but once they had started wanting more than a bit of mild petting she had had no difficulty whatsoever in telling them no.

True, a certain scene in a film or a passage in a book might have the power to make her ache a little—she was human, after all—but she had never allowed herself to experience that ache with a real flesh-and-blood man.

Until last night.

For him. With him.

Keira paced the floor of her hotel room in

agitation. She couldn't stay and work for him. Why not? Because she was afraid that she might end up wanting to go to bed with him? Because she was afraid that she might, as he had taunted her, end up begging him to take her?

No! Where was her pride? Surely she was strong enough not to let that happen? Where was her courage and her self-esteem? Let him say what he liked. She would show him that she meant what she had said. She would remain detached and uninterested in him as a man. Would she? Could she? She was a twenty-seven-year-old virgin who in reality was scared to death she might be in danger of breaking a vow she had made almost a decade ago, and he was a man who looked as though he went through women faster than a monsoon flood went through a rice field.

She mustn't think like that, Keira warned herself. She must remember the old adage that the thought was father to the deed, and not will her own self-destruction on herself.

The hard, cold reality was that she could not afford to lose this contract any more than she could afford to be sexually vulnerable to him. If she blew this, she would never get another opportunity to match it. Chances like this came once in a lifetime—if you were lucky. Her success here would elevate her to a much higher professional status. All she had to do was to keep the promise she had made herself not to allow herself to be physically vulnerable.

At exactly two minutes to eight, Keira walked into the hotel reception area and told the girl on the desk that she was expecting a car to be sent for her.

At five past eight Sayeed came hurrying through the hotel entrance, grinning broadly when he saw her.

'Jay apologises, but he can't make it after all,' he told her as he sank down into the plush vibrant pink cushions of the gilded wood chair opposite her own.

He put the A4 manila envelope he had been carrying down on the marble table in front of them before signalling for a waiter, and then, without asking Keira what she wanted, he ordered champagne for both of them, his dark eyes sparkling with excitement.

'He gave me the contract for you to sign. I'm leaving for Mumbai and then London in the morning, but I'll make sure I get it back to him before I leave. Oh, and he said he'll be in touch with you tomorrow about arranging to bring you up to speed with what's happening and what he's looking for you to provide. It's a great deal, Keira. A good payment in advance that will give you some working capital. One thing I will say for Jay is that he expects the best and he's prepared to pay for it.'

The waiter brought their champagne.

Sayeed picked up his glass and raised it to her in a toast.

'To success.'

Half an hour later the contract was signed and witnessed, Sayeed had promised to fax her a copy once Jay had signed as well—and Keira's head was swimming slightly from the combined effects of champagne and her own awareness that there was now no going back.

CHAPTER FOUR

KEIRA had just finished answering the last of her e-mails when she heard a knock on her hotel room door. Automatically she went to answer it, her body stiffening when she opened the door to find Jay standing there.

When Sayeed had told her that Jay would contact her she had assumed that he would telephone her, not arrive unannounced outside her room at such an early hour of the morning. Immediately she felt on edge and at a disadvantage.

'I thought we'd make an early start so that we can drive out to the site before it gets too hot. Then we can come back and go through what I expect from you and the timing,' Jay told her, stepping into her room so that she had to fall back.

It was a large room, with typical hotel anonymity, but somehow having him inside it with her made Keira acutely conscious of its intimacy and privacy.

'If you'd rung me I could have met you in Reception,' Keira told him sharply.

'If you'd had your mobile on you'd have known that I did ring you—several times,' he countered.

Keira could feel her face going red as she picked up her mobile and realised that he was right. She'd completely overlooked the fact that she'd switched if off when she was with Sayeed in the hotel foyer last night.

'You'll need to wear sensible shoes and a hat,' he told her, causing Keira to grit her teeth.

'Thank you, but I have visited building sites before.'

It wasn't entirely true, but she wasn't going to have him thinking she was totally incapable.

She paused, and then said steadily, 'I can be ready to meet you in the hotel foyer very quickly. It won't take me long to get changed.'

Jay's mouth thinned. Was she daring to hint that she believed he had come to her room because he had some personal interest in her? After all that he had said to her yesterday? Was this yet another of her teasing games, designed to excite male interest? If so she was going to learn that he was not easily excited, and when it came to playing games he always played to win...

'Any man who believes a woman when she tells him that is a fool,' he answered. 'You've got five minutes.' And then, before Keira could object, he had settled himself in a chair and, having reached for the TV remote, was checking the stock market reports.

It took Keira precisely four minutes to get changed—behind her locked bathroom door—into a pair of sand-coloured and very business-like cargo pants, a plain short- sleeved white tee shirt, and a pair of comfortable desert-style trainers.

Emerging from the bathroom, she gathered up a hat, her sunglasses, and a long-sleeved cotton shirt to wear over her tee shirt. She put them into the wicker basket which already held her notepad and some pencils, all without daring to look in the direction of the man seated in front of the TV with his back to her.

She wasn't used to having a man in what was essentially her bedroom. His presence there was making her feel both acutely gauche and even more conscious of him, in a way that somehow caused her thoughts to slip sideways to a place that had her recklessly wondering if he would be watching television whilst he waited for her, if they were lovers who had just spent the night together.

Now her imagination was conjuring up images that made her hands shake, and she felt very glad indeed that he wasn't looking at her. He would sleep naked—but would he hold his lover in his arms after the act of possessing her, keeping her close as he slept? Would she wake to the intimate drift of his hands on her skin and his kiss on her lips? He would be a passionate lover, but would he also possess a tender side?

She would never know, because she would never know any man's passion or tenderness. The starkness of the feeling of loss that descended on her shocked her. She looked at the back of Jay's head, willing the unwanted feeling to disappear.

As she reached for her laptop and put it into the basket, Jay switched off the TV and stood up for all the world as though he had been able to see everything she had done and felt, even though he had had his back to her. It was an unnerving thought.

Five minutes later he was driving them out of the hotel grounds in a sturdy four-by-four, his eyes shaded from the sharp sunlight by a pair of Raybans that made him look even more intimidating than ever.

They turned off the new road that ran from the equally new airport past the old city to the hotel complex onto a rough track, sending up clouds of dust as they went along that made Keira glad of the four-by-four's air-conditioning and comfortable seats.

'How far advanced is the building work?' Keira asked Jay.

'We're pretty close to completion and ahead of schedule at the moment, but that doesn't mean we can afford to relax. We're planning to launch the development well before the monsoon arrives, with TV and other media coverage in Mumbai, and a big event in the hotel, followed up by free look-and-see flights out for prospective buyers. That's why I've stipulated in your contract that I want you based out here, where I can keep a day-to-day overview of your progress and your exclusive services until your contract with us is complete.'

Keira tensed in shock.

'You want me based out here? I can't do that. My office is in London and—'

She gasped as the front wheels of the four-by-four hit a rut, throwing her painfully against her seat belt.

'I'm afraid that you are going to have to be. The contract makes our terms clear. Didn't you read it?'

'I must have missed that bit,' Keira fibbed. She could see from the look he gave her that he didn't believe her. It simply hadn't occurred to her that he would want to oversee her work. If it had…if she had thought for one minute that she would be working closely with him on a day-to-day basis…she would have… She would have what?

Refused the contract? She couldn't afford to financially. But could she afford the emotional cost of the effect he might have on her?

'I'm going to have to go back to London if only to source things,' she told him.

He was looking really angry now.

'It is my express wish that all materials used in the interior design of this development are sourced as locally as possible. That is a key requirement of the contract and a key feature of the project. We have been extremely fortunate in securing both the land and the planning agreement for this project from my brother, the Maharaja, and his granting of that permission was conditional upon us meeting certain set targets with regard to benefits from the project for local people. It is his desire and mine that as a second stage in the redevelopment of Ralapur, the old city itself will become the favoured destination of wealthy cosmopolitan travellers. In order for it to have that appeal it is essential that its unique living history is preserved. Surely Sayeed told you all of this, and informed you that we are working very closely with the Maharaja and his advisers to ensure that his conditions are met? Conditions which, as it happens, I totally support.'

Well, of course he would, seeing as the Maharaja was his brother. He himself was every bit the royal prince, all arrogance and aristocratic pride. No doubt he was used to having his way whenever he wanted it and however he wanted it, with women as well as in business. Well, he wasn't going to have his way with her!

'I can't remember, Your Royal Highness,' Keira lied again, not wanting to get Sayeed into trouble. Normally she would have been filled with admiration for the stance being taken by both the Maharaja and Jay, but on this occasion she was all too conscious of how difficult it would make putting as much distance as possible between Jay and herself.

The look he was giving her was openly contemptuous, as well as grimly angry.

'It is not necessary for you to address me in such a manner. Since I have chosen not to play a role that requires me to use my title, I see no reason why I should be addressed by it.'

Now he had surprised her—but why should that bother her? She wasn't afraid of him, was she? She wasn't afraid that somehow she *would* end up begging him to make love to her? No, of course she wasn't. The very idea was ludicrous, unthinkable. Because if she did then... Her heart had started to pound and a now familiar and very dangerous ache had started to spread slowly but unstoppably through her.

He was driving them up to the top of a steep incline, onto a small plateau, the wheels of the four-by-four were still throwing up clouds of dust, and Keira didn't know what she would have done to stop that ache from spreading if she hadn't suddenly caught her first glimpse of the development site and realised just what it was that Jay was creating.

'You're building a copy of the old city!' she exclaimed in astonishment, as she looked through the dust towards the rose-red sandstone city walls and the open gateway into them, beyond which she could see a mass of buildings and workmen. 'Sayeed said you were building apartments.'

'We are. These are apartments,' he told her, gesturing towards the buildings inside the city wall. 'And once we've finished work on this we'll be building the office blocks that will house the new IT industry on the other side of the new city. The office blocks are going to be mirror-fronted, so that they'll reflect the natural landscape rather than intrude on it, and we're using an up-to-date version of traditional building and design methods where the residential area is concerned. The idea of an ancient city excites everyone's imagination, including mine, so we've decided to see if we can recreate it from the outside whilst making what's inside more suitable for modern-day living, as well as environmentally sound. For instance, the new city will be a car-free area, and each group of homes will share an inner courtyard complete with swimming pool and private family spaces. Flat roofs will be converted into gardens. We want the new community to be serviced as far as possible from within the existing population, rather than bringing in a workforce from outside.'

It was a hugely ambitious project, and Keira could hardly take in the scale of it.

'Ethically it makes good sense,' Keira agreed, 'but you have to consider that the local population may not have the necessary skills. Even if they do, they may not be able to service the demands of a large number of new households.'

'Which is why I am already in discussion with my brother and some of the local family elders with a view to setting up training schemes to be run by skilled local craftsmen to teach the skills that will be needed. By the time the office blocks are ready for occupation, it is my intention that all the necessary infrastructure and practical aspects of comfortable everyday living for the people who will work in them will be in place and working efficiently.'

Jay stopped the car on a dusty expanse of hard flat earth.

'The first phase of the housing development is almost finished. I'll take you over so that you can have a look at them. We'll have to walk from here.'

* * *

Two hours later Keira acknowledged that what she'd been shown was any designer's dream— or nightmare, depending on that designer's self-confidence and the support he or she would get from those in charge of financing the project.

The architecture of the residential area followed that of the old city very closely. The homes were grouped in clusters, each with its own personal, enclosed courtyard garden for privacy, and each grouping also shared a larger courtyard with formal gardens. The houses were mainly two-storey, with large balconies on the first floor and access to a sheltered flat roof space. They were either two- or four-bedroom, and each bedroom had its own bathroom. The master bedroom had a good-sized dressing room.

On the ground floor the smaller two bedroom properties were open plan, with long galley kitchens that could be shut off from the main living area by a folding wall, while the larger properties had separate family-sized kitchens.

Each property had a small office space, and good access onto its courtyard, which was designed to serve as an extra outdoor living space. The concept was both practical and modern, whilst the look of the buildings was traditional, with the houses grouped around what would be an open 'market square'. There was also what looked like a traditional bazaar, but in fact, Jay explained to Keira, it would be a set of buildings housing modern coffee shops and restaurants, as well as shops selling food and other necessary staples.

The houses were to have traditional hard floors, either in marble or mosaic tiles or, for a more modern feel, slate. The look Jay wanted for the interiors, as he had made plain to Keira, was one of simple elegance, in keeping with the whole concept, with a mixture of traditional and modern styles and furnishings to suit the tastes of the eventual purchasers of the properties.

'I want a style for these properties which is unique, conveying a certain status and meeting the aspirations of the people who will live here. It must be individual with regard to each property, and yet at the same time create an overall harmony.'

That would mean using strong key colours that would both harmonise and contrast to produce individuality, whilst keeping to an underlying theme—perhaps with plain off-white walls throughout the interiors, but with very different fabrics and furnishings textures and styles, in a palette of colours. Sharp limes and cool blues, hot pinks and reds, bright yellows and rich golds. Indian colours, but used in ways that transcended the traditional whilst still respecting it.

'I shall need to know if you want each house within a group to share the same style, with each group styled differently, or if you want a mix of styles within each grouping, repeated over several groups,' Keira told Jay.

'You'll be able to see the overall plan more clearly when you see the scale model,' Jay answered her. 'Ultimately we intend to give people both the opportunity to work and live here, or to use it as a leisure facility. We plan to create a lake within walking distance of the development for leisure purposes, which together with the existing lake and hotel—as well, of course, as the attraction of the ancient city—will make this somewhere people want to come and visit, as well as live in. The hotel will be extended to include a facility for corporate entertaining, and we hope with irrigation to be able to source much of the food that will be needed for the new town and the visitors locally.'

Keira was stunned by the breadth of his vision. 'It's a very ambitious project,' was all she could find to say.

'I'm a very ambitious man,' he told her.

And a very sexy man. An unnervingly charismatic and sensually disturbing man. Surely it wasn't possible for the space inside the vehicle to have become smaller, so that she was forced to be more aware of his physical presence as a man? It was the fault of the bright sunlight that she had to turn her head to avoid its glare, and was thus obliged to look at the way his hands held the steering wheel—as knowledgeably and masterfully as he had held her last night.

How had her thoughts managed to slip sideways into that forbidden place she knew they must not go? Keira wondered angrily. It was almost as though her own body was working against her in some way, trying to undermine her.

So what if he was sexy and charismatic and... and sensually disturbing? He was also cruel and unkind and arrogant, incapable of judging her fairly, and she would be a complete fool to let herself be caught in any kind of sexual attraction to him. But wasn't the truth that she was already acutely aware of him as a man?

Keira could feel her heart thumping. She must not give in to this unfamiliar and unwanted vulnerability.

'There's a fabric designer whose fabrics might work well here,' she told Jay, putting aside her personal concerns to focus on her work. 'He might be prepared to design and produce some fabrics specifically to order for us. What I'm thinking of is using the hot colours India is famous for, but in a more modern way—stripes and checks, perhaps, in thick hessian and slubbed linen, coarse cottons rather than sheer silks. Fabrics that have a modern appeal to them but still an Indian feel. We could have light fittings in coloured mosaic glass, but in modern shapes.'

Her own imagination was taking fire now, leaping ahead of her, illuminating the way just as the mosaic glass lanterns she was visualising would illuminate the cool shadows of enclosed courtyard gardens and rooms.

The fabrics she was envisaging would work just as well with modern pared-down minimalist furniture in plastic and chrome as they would with more ornate traditional things.

She was as fiercely passionate about her work as he was, Jay recognised reluctantly. He didn't want to acknowledge that they shared a certain mind-set, he didn't want to find that he admired her professionalism, and he certainly didn't want to have to admit even to himself that he had actually enjoyed talking to her about his vision for the future of this development because he had sensed that, unlike so many other women he had known, she was genuinely interested in what he was doing.

Instead he focused on the sensuality of the

way she talked about her work. It was like watching an image come to life, her passion illuminating her expression. The same way she herself would come to life in his arms in the heat of passion, offering him her body and her pleasure, inciting him to take it and to take her, exciting and denying him until he was driven to possess her in every way imaginable.

His body tightened with a desire he had to punish her for causing.

'You paint a very sensual picture. Deliberately so, I suspect.' His voice was harsh and accusatory.

'I was simply describing a light fitting. If you choose to see something sensual in that then that is up to you.' Keira defended herself even whilst her heart thudded into her ribs.

'You did not consider it sensual yourself? There are those who believe that the underlying message of the *Kama Sutra* is that everything we are is designed for sexual and sensual pleasure.'

The shock caused by his words sent a sharp thrill zig-zagging down her spine, as though he had actually touched her there himself. She could feel the warmth of his breath heating her skin, just as his words were heating her already fevered imagination.

The *Kama Sutra*! It was unfair, surely, that he should refer to a such a book after what he had said to her about her having to beg him for sex? Was he deliberately trying to test her?

'I wouldn't know,' she told him sharply. 'It isn't a book I've ever felt any inclination to read.' There—that should make it plain to him that she was sticking firmly to business.

'Because you don't feel you have anything to learn from it?'

'Books instructing women to debase themselves for a man's pleasure will never be something I'd want to learn from,' Keira hit back.

'The *Kama Sutra* contains no suggestion of debasement of anyone. Rather it is about the honing of mutual pleasure, the giving and taking of that pleasure, the sensual and sexual education of both male and female so that they can experience the greatest degree of mutual pleasure with and for one another. I am surprised that you did not know that.'

If she could have walked away from him she would have done so, Keira knew. Anything to get away from the taunting softness of that male voice, painting images inside her head that made her ache as though her whole body was on fire. Images which had no right to be there and which she did not *want* to be there.

'It's time for us to head back.'

His abrupt change of subject was a relief, but Keira still felt it wise to keep her distance from him as they headed back towards the four-by-four over the rutted and rock-strewn ground. He was walking very fast, his longer legs carrying him over the rough ground far more swiftly than her own, and in her haste not to look unprofessional and helpless she started to walk faster, ignoring the danger in the loose rocks and deep gulleys carved into the dusty road by the wheels of heavy excavation plant.

They had almost reached the four-by-four when it happened. A loose stone beneath her foot rolled away into one of the gulleys, causing her to lose her balance.

Jay heard Keira's exclamation of alarm and

turned back, moving swiftly towards her, reaching her just in time to catch her as she stumbled.

His chest was on a level with her eyes and Keira could see its fierce rise and fall. It mesmerised her as much as the hot male scent of his body, sending out a message that locked on to her own female hormones, dizzying and almost drugging them with awareness of his masculinity. She could feel the heat of the sun on her back, but it was as nothing compared to the heat burning through her from the grip of Jay's hands on her arms.

All he was doing was steadying her. She knew that. But to her body his hold was dangerously reminiscent of the way he had held her when he had kissed her, and she had to fight down its instinctive urge to close the gap between them. If he kissed her now he would taste of salt and heat and male hormones…

It must be the shock of her unwanted sexual response to him that was responsible for the feeling that somehow time had slowed down, and with it the beat of her own heart, as though both of them were caught up in some kind of mystical spell, Keira thought dizzily. She could see where the shadow was just beginning to darken the line of Jay's jaw, and she had an overwhelming longing to reach out and touch it with her fingertips, and then to trace the curve of his mouth. The sensuality of the contrast between them would, she knew, be burned into her touch in a way that would make her ache to feel that contrast against her own flesh. It would be so easy to do, so very easy.

He knew what she was doing, Jay assured himself. She was trying to use his own maleness against him, knowing what effect her proximity would have on him. He had never known a woman so skilled at using his own sexuality against him. Where other women were foolish enough to blatantly thrust themselves on him, for him to either take or repulse as his mood dictated, she was far more subtle and skilled. Dangerously so, he recognised grimly, since her subtle waiting game had already resulted in arousing him. He shouldn't have referred to the *Kama Sutra,* Jay acknowledged. Doing so had conjured up images inside his head that had weakened his defences: images of sensuality and love-play in which her pale naked body was his to arouse and enjoy.

If he kissed her now…

Panicked by what she was thinking—and feeling—Keira told herself that it was relief she felt when Jay removed his hands from her arms and she was free to step back from him. What was wrong with her? Didn't she recognise her own danger and how foolish it was for her to keep having these wholly inappropriate and unwanted thoughts? It was as though some stranger had taken possession of her, and she was no longer in control of her own thoughts and feelings.

'Thanks,' she told him huskily, striving to appear normal, but avoiding looking directly at him.

She had done it again, Jay thought grimly. She had aroused him and then walked away. No woman did that to him and got away with it—especially not this one.

CHAPTER FIVE

'ONCE you've seen the scale model of the project, I'd like to see some concrete plans and sketches for the interiors for the first phase of the apartments as soon as possible,' Jay told Keira crisply as he drove them back down the dusty untarmacked road.

He had removed his sunglasses now that they were no longer driving into the sun, but the light was still too bright for Keira to want to remove her own.

'I'm leaving for Mumbai tomorrow evening, which will give you just over twenty-four hours to come up with an overview for me before I leave.'

The speed at which he expected her to work was shocking.

'I can't possibly produce detailed interior

plans in twenty-four hours,' Keira protested, her face burning slightly as she sensed from the sideways look he slashed towards her that he was taking her words as an admission of failure rather than as an honest professional assessment of what could be accomplished in such a limited time span. Well, she wasn't going to recall or deny them. Her chin lifted, and the look she returned to him said without words that she wasn't going to recant—or apologise.

Keira could almost feel his mind probing her silence and assessing it. Her chin tilted a bit higher, but she wasn't going to risk looking directly into those platinum-grey eyes. Just thinking about the power of their uncompromisingly analytical surveillance made her feel far too weak. Platinum. One of the most desired and valuable metals in today's world. Somehow the colour of his eyes was symbolic of the man himself.

'Overviews, I said—not detailed plans,' Jay informed her coolly. 'Themes, colours, some take on style, so that I can mull them over whilst I'm travelling.'

'I haven't got my samples with me, or a proper office, or…'

'You'll be staying in the guest wing of the palace whilst you're working on this project. I've already arranged for the hotel to shift your stuff over to it, so it should be waiting for you when we get back. The accommodation provided for you includes an office.'

As easily as the first Mughal warriors had taken possession of the land, he had cut the ground from beneath her feet.

Oblivious to the bombshell he had just dropped on her, Jay continued briskly, 'You'll find it much more convenient, being in the city, and I'll supply you with a driver so that you can go out to the site if you need to whilst I'm in Mumbai. As for your samples—I thought I'd already made it clear that I expect you to use locally sourced materials. I'll take you down to the bazaar once I've shown you the scale model of the site, and introduce you to some of the suppliers I've already sourced.'

'Are you sure that you *want* a designer?' The thought of having to share a living space with him had upset her so much that Keira was in a headlong flight that redirected her fear into sarcasm. 'It seems to me that what you really want is someone who says yes to everything you say.'

'Isn't that what all women secretly want?' Jay taunted her softly. 'A man who can tame her creativity to fit his own desires and tells her so? You modern women may deny it, but none of us can go against nature. Isn't it true that secretly you prefer a man to know himself and his desires so that he can use them to become a truly creative and imaginative lover, who can take you to a place where every fantasy you've ever had can be fulfilled? Be honest and admit that it's true. A woman of your age living in these modern times must know that truth—unless, of course, you are still waiting for a man with whom you can experience that degree of pleasure.'

How was it possible for her to feel so hot and so cold at the same time, with her stomach churning with shocked fear and her head dizzy with even more shocked excitement?

'Nothing to say? Perhaps, then, the lovers

you've experienced in the past weren't as satisfying as they might have been?'

What was going on? How had the conversation managed to go from a businesslike discussion of Jay's requirements to this? However it had happened, it certainly wasn't kindly intentioned, Keira suspected.

She took a deep breath and told him calmly, 'I don't think that this kind of conversation is appropriate, given our business relationship.'

She was doing it again. Jay could feel the heat of mingled anger and arousal beating up inside his body, threatening his self-control. He had no idea what it was about this woman that pushed against the boundaries of that control and threatened it so dramatically and with such speed, but he couldn't deny any more that there was something about her that did. It acted on him like a goad—irritating, driving, inciting, making him burn with a need to make her want him as much as he did her, to make her admit that want and cry it out to him. Only then could his pride be salved. Only her pleas for his possession and her cries of pleasure could satisfy it. And him?

'Not given our business relationship,' he agreed. 'But what about *this* relationship?'

As he finished speaking he took his hand off the steering wheel, reached out slowly, and very deliberately rubbed his thumb across Keira's nipple.

The shock of his touch was like an electric charge shooting through her. Her body, already sensitised to him from their earlier intimacy, reacted with the immediacy of a monsoon downpour, drenching her with aching need.

One look at her blatantly aroused expression had Jay stopping the four-by-four abruptly in the middle of the dusty empty road. It was almost midday, and there was no escape for anyone foolish enough to be caught in the sun's heat as it scorched the scrubby patches of dried-out grass. In the distance Keira could see trees that would provide shade and protection from the heat. But, like the grass, she was exposed by her own foolishness, and there was no protection for her unless she herself created it. She could feel the heat pressing in on the four-by-four as though trying to possess and overwhelm its artificial air-conditioned coolness. Safety and security were such fragile things when they were opposed by the forces of nature. But they still had to be fought and an effort made to control them.

Her breasts ached heavily, her nipples hard with longing for what they couldn't have.

'That isn't a relationship,' she told Jay flatly. 'It's…it's…'

'Desire…need…hunger…'

Keira could feel her control being stolen from her.

'It's nothing,' she corrected him.

'Nothing? Are you sure?'

'You've hired me as an interior designer. That is the only relationship I want there to be between us.'

Keira held her breath, waiting for him to call her a liar.

'Your body tells a different story. No doubt because it is well trained to react to my sex in a way that flatters it.'

He was being brutally insulting, but Keira wasn't going to give him the satisfaction of seeing that he had upset her. Instead she told him coolly, 'It's amazing how often what we think we recognise in other people is merely what we have already decided we *want* to recognise.'

The look he gave her made her heart thud and then race with the fear of the hunted for the hunter. Within seconds she knew why.

'Are you saying that the telltale hardness of your nipples was caused specifically by me and for me?'

His challenge had caught her in a trap of her own making, and there was nothing she could do now other than look straight ahead and tell him in a betrayingly constricted voice, 'I think we should change the subject.'

This was a new variation on an old game, Jay acknowledged, and it was certainly an unexpectedly excitingly erotic one. She was good. She was very good. She could turn him from pride to anger, and from that to sexual heat and desire, all within the space of a few minutes and a handful of words. If she was as good in bed…

* * *

Half an hour later the four-by-four was parked in the city car park and they were being welcomed back into the very grand entrance hall Keira remembered from the previous day.

The scale model of the new city and its planned surrounding development was displayed on a large table under glass in an otherwise almost empty room, down the corridor and past Jay's office.

A man who had the ambition and the wealth to underwrite this kind of project had to have a determined and even a ruthless side to his nature, Keira acknowledged. He would certainly make a very formidable opponent, and one who would never willingly accept defeat or being denied something he wanted.

Without any orders seeming to be given, a houseboy had appeared with tea, and Keira drank the hot reviving liquid gratefully.

'We'll eat in the old town whilst we're out,' Jay told her. 'There are several good restaurants there. Meanwhile, if you want to freshen up, Kunal here will show you to your quarters.'

He raised his wrist to look at his watch, and un-wittingly Keira looked too.

His forearm was firmly muscled, its olive skin darkened with body hair. A feeling that was a volatile mix of weakness and heat flipped her heart against her ribs and tightened her lower stomach muscles. What was happening to her? How could just looking at a man's wrist do something like this to her? Have her imagining him pinning her down against the softness of a voile-curtained bed with the weight of that arm over her naked body?

'I've got a couple of phone calls to make, so I'll meet you downstairs in half an hour.'

Keira was glad that all she needed to do was nod her head and then turn to follow the houseboy, because she simply didn't trust herself to speak.

The guest wing must originally have been the women's quarters of the palace, Keira guessed. It had its own enclosed courtyard garden, complete with a fountain and a pool which she could see and hear through the open arched windows from the enormous bedroom Kunal had shown her to.

'You like?' Kunal asked her shyly. 'This palace was built many many years ago by the Maharaja. Ralapur has many palaces—all very beautiful.'

'Ralapur reminds me of Jaipur,' Keira told him.

'No,' Kunal told her vehemently, immediately shaking his head. 'Ralapur is better than Jaipur. Much better.' He was laughing now, inviting her to share in his joke and his loyalty to his home.

Keira waited until Kunal had gone before exploring her new quarters. The bedroom had a hugely ornate French empire-style bed, which looked as though it had been built and decorated specifically for the room, and the bathroom, reached via a door to one side of the bed was virtually the same size as the whole of her open-plan living space in her London apartment, decadently opulent with a sunken bath and mirrored walls.

These rooms had been created for a sexually active and sensual woman, Keira decided—a woman who had been a courtesan, surely, rather than a consort? Was that why he had given her this suite? As a reminder of what he considered her to be?

She washed and changed quickly into a cotton top with short sleeves and a softly pleated skirt, and then made her way back along the corridor and down the stairs to the hallway, where Jay was standing waiting for her.

'I thought we would eat here,' Jay announced, indicating the fretted arched doorway of a restaurant just off the city's main street.

'They serve traditional local food, and I should warn you that it is quite spicy. If you would prefer to eat somewhere else…?'

Keira hadn't thought that she was hungry, but just the smell of food wafting through the door was enough to make her mouth water.

'No—here is fine,' she assured him.

The restaurant was busy, with waiters wearing brightly coloured traditional clothes and intricately folded turbans that gave them a fierce warrior-like air, and diners seated on large cushions on the floor around low-level tables.

Everyone turned to look at Jay, no doubt

because of his status as a member of the royal family. The waiters bowed low to him, and the restaurant owner, who was dressed in a European business suit, came hurrying forward to welcome them, offering them a higher table with chairs when he saw Keira.

But Keira shook her head. 'Unless, of course, you would prefer that?' she asked Jay.

His dismissive shrug said that it wasn't a matter of any great concern to him how they sat, and he certainly had no trouble whatsoever adopting the traditional almost yoga-type pose she had assumed herself, with her legs and feet covered by her skirt.

'We serve traditional smoked *sule kebas* here,' the owner informed her, 'and the vegetarian food of the Maheshwari of the Marwaris. But if I may, I would recommend our *dal baati,* which is a house speciality.'

'Yes, please,' Keira accepted with a smile.

She was certainly at ease with traditional India customs and food, Jay acknowledged, as he watched Keira eating her meal with obvious enjoyment.

The shops were just reopening after the heat of the day when they stepped back out into the wide tree-shaded avenue, just over an hour later.

Jay explained to her that the water supply came from artesian wells deep down in the earth, below the rocky plateau on which the city was built and that the seventeenth-century poet prince who had created the city had had underground storage systems built to provide water not just for his palace and his city but also for his gardens.

Listening to Jay, Keira could hear in his voice the pride in his ancestor. Their backgrounds were so very different. He could take pride in his parents and his upbringing, where all she could feel was shame. He was the son of a Maharaja; she was the daughter of a prostitute and a drug addict. He was a man and she was a woman, and when he touched her. But, no—she must not think like that.

Children in uniform were filing out of their school, walking together in pairs in a sedate crocodile.

'My brother has instituted several reforms

since he came to power,' Jay told Keira as they watched the children. 'One of which is to ensure that every child receives a good education. He says it's the best investment there can be, as these children will be the future not just of our city but of India itself.'

They had reached the entrance to the bazaar and Keira stood still, its sights and scents enveloping her. Bright silks hung in the doorway of one shop, whilst intricately hand-beaten metalware lay heaped on the pavement outside another. A jeweller was throwing back his shutters to reveal the brightness of his gold to the late-afternoon sunshine. From inside a herbalist's shop the pungent smell of his goods drifted out into the heat.

Children released from their crocodile darted up the narrow passageways, laughing to one another, whilst three young Hindu initiates passed by in their orange robes, their voices raised in chanting joy.

Several hours later, when they were in the shop of a fabric merchant, Keira had to admit that Jay had sourced his contacts well. The merchant had told them that he had cousins who owned and ran a factory in a small town, south-east of the city, a town Keira already knew was famous for its block-printed cotton. The town owed its success to the fact that a local stream possessed certain minerals in its water that set dye.

The merchant had produced pattern books, showing some classic floral and pineapple designs originating from the eighteenth century, and others showing fabrics in indigo and madder, as well as assuring her that his cousins would be pleased to make up samples of fabrics for her in her own choice of colours.

The merchant's daughter-in-law came through from the living quarters at the rear of the shop, bringing tea for them to drink, with two young children clinging to her sari. The younger of them, a little girl with huge dark-brown eyes and soft curls, was only just learning to walk, and when she lost her balance Keira reacted immediately, catching her in her arms to steady her. Was there anything quite as wonderful as holding a child? Keira wondered tenderly as the little girl looked up and smiled shyly at her. A sense of loss filled her. There wouldn't ever be any children of her own for her.

Jay watched Keira with the fabric merchant's grandchild, and, seeing the look on her face, wondered what had caused it. Why was he so curious about her? She meant nothing to him, and that was the way he intended things to stay.

The fabric merchant was telling Keira that if she were to let him have some drawings and details of what she wanted he could arrange to have some sample patterns made up for her. Keira handed the little girl back to her mother and reached for her notebook and the samples, swiftly selecting colours and patterns in the combinations she thought she would need, her manner now businesslike and focused.

She had a easy rapport with people and a natural way of communicating with them, Jay observed. She respected their professionalism, and he could see that they in turn respected hers.

It was very important to him that this new

venture was not just a success, but that it achieved an almost iconic status as a leader in its field. His heritage and his blood demanded that from him, as much as his own nature and pride.

Jay knew that there were those who envied him his success and would like to see him fail, but they never would. He was determined about that. He never lost—at anything. And this woman was going to learn that just as his business rivals had had to learn it.

And yet, despite the fact that on a personal level Keira pushed all the wrong buttons for him, as a designer he couldn't fault her. Somehow, without him being able to analyse just how she was doing it, she was creating an image for the properties that truly was cosmopolitan and yet at the same time very much of India. He had almost been able to see it taking shape in front of him as she talked to suppliers and merchants, her slender fingers reaching for small pots of paint and dye, or pieces of fabric, her quick mind picking up ideas and then translating them to those with whom she was dealing.

Professionally she was, as Sayeed had said, perfect for this commission.

Keira thanked the fabric merchant for his help, and got up from the cushion on which she had been seated whilst they talked with the single fluid movement she had learned from Shalini, ignoring the hand Jay had stretched out to help her. The last thing she wanted was to risk any physical contact with him, even if by doing so she was causing his mouth to tighten and earning herself a grim look. She couldn't think of a commission she would enjoy more than the one he had given her—it was a dream come true, and all the more so now that she had met the suppliers he had already sourced—but Jay's presence made that dream a nightmare.

He was going away tomorrow, she reminded herself, and she was going to be working so hard that she simply wouldn't have time to think about him, much less worry about her vulnerability to him.

It had grown dark whilst they had been in the shop, and now the street outside was illuminated with pretty glass lamps. The street opened into a small square where several men sat at a table enjoying *shiska* pipes, the bright colours of their turbans glowing under the light from the lanterns.

A group of young female dancers wearing traditional dress, followed by several musicians, swirled through the square, on their way to one of the restaurants to dance for the diners, Keira guessed.

The evening air was vibrant with the scents, sights and sounds of India. They throbbed and pulsed in the warm air, taking on their own life form—a life form that was softened and gentled by the nature of the people.

Jay had stopped to talk to a tall man in a western suit who had hailed him. Whilst they were talking Keira spotted an antique shop on the other side of the square and quickly headed toward it. Antiques and bric-a-brac were something she just couldn't resist.

A tall boy, a teenager, dark-eyed and with the promise of handsomeness to come—was obviously minding the shop for someone else, and welcomed her in shyly. He couldn't be more than seventeen or eighteen at the most, Keira assessed, and whilst he was looking at her with curiosity, she didn't feel offended or threatened. He probably wasn't used to seeing Western women, and she knew he meant no harm.

The shop contained mainly bric-a-brac, and she was on the point of leaving when she saw a box full of black and white photographs on one of the shelves. She went to pick it up but the boy beat her to it, standing very close to her as he reached for the box for her.

Taking it from him, Keira looked through the photographs, her excitement growing as she did so. The box contained a mix of postcard pictures of maharajas and palaces, and so far as she was concerned was a terrific find. Properly framed they would make wonderful and highly individual wall art for the properties.

'How much for all of these?' she asked the boy, gesturing to the box.

'For you, lovely lady, is one thousand rupees,' he told her.

Keira knew the rules of trade here, and so she shook her head and told him firmly, 'Too much.'

Then she offered him less than half of what he had asked for.

'No—is a good price I give you,' the boy told her earnestly, moving closer to her as though to reinforce his point. 'Because I like you. You are very pretty. Are you here on holiday?' he asked her. 'Do you have a boyfriend?'

Keira's heart sank. Oh, dear. Perhaps she should have been prepared for this, but she hadn't been.

'Perhaps I should come back later—' she began, but to her consternation the boy grabbed hold of her arm.

'No, please stay,' he begged her. 'I will give you the photographs if you like them.'

This was even worse, and Keira didn't know what she would have done if a man Keira assumed must be the boy's father and Jay hadn't arrived in the shop at the same time, neither of them looking very pleased.

'What's going on?' Jay demanded.

'I was just trying to buy these photographs,' Keira told him, unwilling to get the boy into trouble.

Very quickly Jay concluded the sale and

handed over the necessary rupees, before hustling her out into the street, rich now with the smell of cooking food from the stalls that had been set up around the square.

Keira could tell that he was angry, but she wasn't prepared for the storm that broke over her the minute they were back inside the palace.

'You just can't resist, can you?' he challenged her savagely. 'Not even with a boy who's still wet behind the ears. The way you were flirting with him was—'

The lanterns illuminating the hallway threw long dark shadows across it. Keira would have given a great deal to hide herself in those shadows, and so escape from the tension between them, but she couldn't let his accusation stand.

'I wasn't flirting with him,' she told him truthfully, defending herself.

'Of course you were. You were leading him on. Just like you—' Jay stopped abruptly, but Keira knew what he had been about to say. He had been about to say just like she had led *him* on.

Shame burned its hot brand on her pale skin, making her cheeks sting.

She could not defend herself against that accusation. Her shame intensified.

'I expect the people who work for me and with me to reflect a proper professional attitude.'

'I *was* being professional,' Keira insisted.

'Yes, and it was perfectly obvious which profession it was you were representing.'

Keira could feel nausea burning her throat, and angry fear flooding her heart. She knew exactly what he was accusing her of being, and which profession he was alluding to: the oldest profession in the world, the profession whereby a woman sold her body to a man for his sexual gratification. Her mother's profession. The profession she had always sworn she would rather die a virgin than risk following.

'I was simply trying to buy the photographs, that was all,' she told Jay fiercely.

Her teeth had started to chatter, despite the fact that it was warm. The sickening fear she had never been able to subdue surged through her, smothering logic and reason. Somewhere deep inside herself the child who had heard her mother's words as though they were a curse on her still cowered under the burden of those words.

The present slipped away from her, leaving her vulnerable to the past and its pain. She could feel it gripping her and refusing to let her go.

The way the colour suddenly left her face and the bruised darkness of her eyes caught Jay off guard. She was looking at him as though he had tried to destroy her. Looking at him and yet somehow past him, as though he simply wasn't there, he recognised. He had never seen such an expression of tormented anguish.

He took a step towards her, but immediately she turned and almost ran up the stairs, fleeing from him as though he was the devil incarnate. Unwanted male guilt mingled with his anger as that very maleness made it a matter of honour for him to let her go, rather than pursue her and demand an explanation for her behaviour.

CHAPTER SIX

SHE had worked like someone possessed from the minute she had closed the door of the guest wing behind her, focusing all her energy on what had to be achieved and deliberately leaving nothing to spare that might trap her with the ghosts Jay's accusation had raised.

But they were still there, pushing against the tight lid of the coffin she had sealed them into like the undead, denied true oblivion and existing in a half world that made them desperate to escape. And it was Jay's words to her that had fed them and given them the strength to try to overpower her.

She looked down at her laptop and at the work she had just completed. Images of room layouts lay printed off and neatly stacked to one side of the laptop—rooms with walls painted in traditionally made paint in subtly different but toning shades of white. In the main she'd opted for modern, stylish furniture in black, chrome and natural wood, accenting the rooms with fabrics in colour palettes that went from acid lemon and lime through to hot sizzling pinks and reds, and from cool greys and blues through to creams and browns. Modern lighting and the use of mirrors opened up the smaller spaces and highlighted features. It was, Keira knew, probably the most complex portfolio she had ever produced at such short notice.

It was late—nearly three o'clock in the morning. She ought to go to bed, but she knew she wasn't relaxed enough to sleep.

Outside, the courtyard garden was bathed in the light from the almost full moon. Keira got up and opened the door that led to it.

The night air was softly warm, without the stifling heat that would come later in the year at the height of summer.

A mosaic-tiled path led to a square pool in the centre of the garden, and surrounded it, and Keira paused to look down at it, studying it more closely.

* * *

Jay couldn't sleep.

He threw back the bedclothes and stood up. He should have followed his initial feeling and brought in another designer—preferably one who was male.

He walked over to the high-arched windows of his room, which he'd left open to the fresh air. Beyond them was an enclosed balcony that ran the whole length of the suite of rooms that had belonged to the Maharaja for whom this palace had originally been built.

This was the only place in the palace from which it was possible to look down not only into his own private courtyard garden but also into that attached to the old women's quarters. Naturally only the Maharaja himself had been allowed to look on the beauty of his wives and concubines. For any other man to do so would have been an offence for which at one time he would have had to pay with his sight and probably his life.

Now no modern man would dream of thinking that no one else should look upon the face of a woman with whom he was involved. A woman was a human being of equal status, not a possession, and the very idea was barbaric—and yet within every man there was still a fierce need to keep to himself the woman he desired, and an equally fierce anger when that need was crossed.

As his had been earlier, when he had seen the way the young shop boy had looked at Keira and the way she had smiled back at him?

That was ridiculous. She meant nothing to him. Just because she had aroused him physically... He stepped out onto the veranda and frowned as he saw a movement in the women's courtyard.

Keira. What was she doing out there at three o'clock in the morning? And why was she crouching on the ground?

Snakes sometimes slid into these gardens.

It only took him a handful of seconds to pull on his underwear and a pair of jeans. The tiles beneath his bare feet still held the warmth of the day's sun as he padded down the private staircase that led into the courtyards. It wasn't until he had opened the gate between his own courtyard and the women's courtyard that Jay realised that what had brought him here had been an age-old in-built male protective concern, which he had not even realised he possessed until now, and which if he had known he possessed, he would not have thought would be activated by or for Keira…

The sight of Jay walking towards her through the shadows was so unexpected that it shocked Keira into immobility for a few seconds, before she struggled to her feet. His terse, 'What are you doing?' didn't help.

'I wanted a closer look at the pattern on these tiles,' she told him, indicating the tiles forming the narrow footpath. 'And if you've come to find out if I've finished the layouts you wanted, then the answer is yes. At least in draft form. They'll be on your desk before you leave tomorrow.'

The words were a staccato burst of edgy defensiveness that fell away into sharp silence when Jay stepped out of the shadows. Automatically she looked at him, and then couldn't look away, her breath locking in her throat, her stomach tightening in response to what she could see. His torso and his feet were bare, as though… as though he had been in bed. Naked? Why was she thinking that? He could just have been relaxing. But something told her that Jay wasn't the kind of man who relaxed by taking off his clothes and lounging around semi-nude.

'If they're ready I may as well have them now,' Jay told her.

'I was going to polish them a bit more.'

'There's no need. It's understood that these are preliminary drafts. If I have them now it will give me more time to consider them. I'll walk back with you and collect them.'

Keira wished she hadn't said anything about the layouts. She'd wanted to look them over again before handing them to him, but now if she refused to let him take them he was bound to think that she'd been boasting, and that they weren't finished at all.

'Very well,' she agreed.

She'd closed her door when she came out. As they approached it Jay stepped in front of her—

intending, she realised too late, to open the door for her. But the practical whys and wherefores of how she had come to be touching him hardly mattered. Because when she'd reached out to stop herself from colliding with him he had reached out too, and now his hand was on her shoulder, and her senses were filled by the feel of his warm flesh beneath her hand and the scent of his skin in her nostrils.

She could have moved away. She certainly should have done so. But instead she was looking up at him, and he was looking back at her. A dangerous tension stretched the silence. Her fingers curled into his arm, the breath shuddering from her lungs.

Danger crackled through her senses like static electricity. Abruptly she removed her hand from his arm, but it was too late. Without knowing that she was doing so she had moved closer to him, as though in mute invitation, and he had responded to that invitation.

She had thought that people only kissed like this in films—briefly, testing, tasting. Two people who were both trying desperately not to give in to the fierce undertow of a desire that neither of them really wanted, only to be swamped by it as their lips met and they were overwhelmed by a hunger that leapt from nerve-ending to nerve-ending, binding them together as their mouths and hands and bodies meshed, plundered and pleaded.

It was like being possessed by a universal force that could not be controlled, Keira thought dizzily, her lips clinging to Jay's. His hand was spread across the back of her head beneath her hair, keeping her mouth close to his own whilst his tongue probed the soft willingness of her mouth, possessing it in the same way that her desire for him was possessing her.

Each intimacy between them only fed her desire for more, as though some powerful spell had been cast upon her ability to resist what was happening to her.

The hunger he had unleashed within her was enslaving her. He was enslaving her, Keira realised as she tried desperately to pull back from the chasm awaiting her and the darkness she knew it held. Only to fail when Jay touched her breast, cupping it within the hold of his hand so that her nipple rose tightly and eagerly to press against his flesh. Keira knew that it was her own response that had incited the explicitly erotic pluck of his fingertips against her nipple as he teased it into an even more blatantly hungry demand for more.

It was like being savaged by two opposing forces. No—it was like being fought over by them, Keira thought frantically. The one surging through her, taking her up to the heights of sexual excitement and need, and the other dragging her down to that place when the demons of her childhood lay in wait for her. Between them they could so easily tear her apart and destroy her. She must stop this. But she couldn't.

Jay was kissing the side of her neck, sending wild, wanton shivers of irreversible arousal racking her. She could hear herself moaning as she collapsed into him, letting him take the weight of her body, letting him know without words of her need for him to possess it and her completely.

He was hard and ready against her softness.

Automatically she reached down between them to touch him, driven now by nature, which guided her movements so that her fingertips fluttered helplessly against the thick hard ridge of his erection.

His smothered groan into her skin followed by the sharply sexual nip of his teeth would have been enough to melt any resistance she might have had, even without the sudden fierce sweep of his free hand down the length of her body, pressing her into him before closing on the soft curve of her buttock.

She was lost, Keira admitted to herself. There could be no going back from this.

In the moonlight she could see the darkness of Jay's hand against her top. As though it was happening in slow motion she watched as his fingers curled into the fabric and pulled it away from her breast. Her heart was thumping slowly and heavily as she silently willed him not to stop, but instead to hurry, hurry... Because the need inside her could not be contained for much longer.

As though he had sensed that need Jay bent

his head, taking her nipple into his mouth with fierce impatience and drawing on it, so that she could feel the sharp pangs of her own desire seizing her whole body, causing it to convulse with longing.

She was his. Jay could sense her body open to his, could already imagine what it would be like when she closed down on him as her orgasm possessed her and took him to his own pleasure. Just thinking about it made him ache so badly. Jay's hand went to the fastening of his jeans. He wanted her so much, was so out of control with longing for her that he doubted he would have time to make it to the bed, never mind anything else.

Anything else? What the hell was happening to him? Jay never allowed himself to be out of control, and he certainly never had unprotected sex. But he had been about to do so.

Had been.

At first when Jay pushed her away Keira couldn't understand or accept what was happening. She cried out in protest, her eyes wild with longing and incomprehension, until she was jerked back to reality by the stillness of Jay's stance and the look she saw in his eyes before he turned on his heel and walked away from her.

Shame, her familiar and hated companion, slid its dark shadow next to her and smiled its mocking triumph at her.

Somehow Keira managed to stumble inside her room, where she showered in darkness, unable to bear the sight of her own body. Her mother and her great-aunt had been right about her after all.

After an hour of lying rigidly in her bed, unable to sleep, she got up and switched on her laptop. But for once her work did not bring its normal comfort, pushing everything and everyone else out of her thoughts. Instead images of Jay—his face, his eyes, his hands— came between her and the screen to torment her.

It was close to dawn when she eventually fell into an exhausted and troubled sleep.

It was just gone six in the morning. Jay was showered and dressed and drinking the tea his manservant had brought him. The morning sun was bathing everything in primrose-gold light, the clear blue of the sky on the horizon turning darker where it met the pink walls of the buildings.

He could admire the city's beauty, but he could not feel entirely a part of it, Jay acknowledged. His self-imposed exile had broadened his horizons too much. The city would always hold a very special place in his heart, but he did not envy his elder brother his inheritance or his position. The status of second son—second best, as his father's mistress had so often taunted him in the past—brought with it a freedom Rao could never have, and in a variety of different ways. He had lost count of the number of approaches he had received in recent years from families desperate to secure him as a husband for their daughters, but unlike Rao he did not have to marry and secure the succession. He was free to remain free, and that was exactly what he intended to do.

He would be leaving within the hour by helicopter to his private jet and his journey to Mumbai.

On the table in front of him were Keira's

plans. He had ordered a servant to retrieve them from her room. There were a couple of points he wanted to query with her before he left. The excellence of what she had done had caught him off guard. Like his loss of control and his reaction to her last night?

He had not lost control. Maybe not completely, but the extent to which he had come dangerously close to doing so had been a first for him. Irritated by the mocking tone of his inner voice, Jay put down his teacup.

The courtyard beneath his window looked so tranquil this morning it was hard to imagine that last night it had contained so much dark passion. A passion instigated by her, when she had taken that inviting step toward him. Maybe—but it was an invitation he could have refused.

He looked at his watch. It was still early, but there were a couple of questions he needed to ask Keira about her plans before he left.

As he stepped outside, the morning sunlight burnished the olive warmth of his skin, throwing into relief the strength of his facial bone structure.

The door to Keira's quarters opened easily. Jay could hear the quiet hum of her laptop and smell the scent of her sleep and her skin. Through the open doorway he could see the bed, and Keira herself, lying on top of it and quite obviously still asleep.

Jay turned back to the door, only to stop and turn again, to walk slowly towards the bed as through drawn there against his will.

Keira was lying on her side, clad in a pair of pyjamas that looked more suitable in design for a girl than a woman, and he could see quite clearly the tracks of her dried tears on her face, below telltale mascara smudges.

She'd been crying? Because of him?

Deep down within himself Jay could feel something, a sensation of emotional tightness and tension, as though something was breaking apart to reveal something else so sensitive and raw that he couldn't bear to feel it.

What was it? Compassion? Pity? Regret? Why should he feel pain for her vulnerability and her tears?

Angry with himself, Jay turned away from the bed and left as silently as he had arrived.

Women used their tears in exactly the same way as they used their bodies: to get what they wanted. He wasn't about to be taken in by such tactics.

Jay had gone and she was safe. Because without his presence she could not be tormented and tempted as she had been last night.

But Jay would come back, and when he did…

When he did things would be different, Keira promised herself grimly. She would have found a way to protect herself from her own weakness. It wasn't her pride that was insisting that she did that. Given the chance, she'd have preferred to run from what Jay aroused in her rather than battle with it. But she simply did not have that freedom. Her contract tied her to the work she had taken on and through that to Jay, and she was not in a position to risk the financial implications of breaking that contract.

CHAPTER SEVEN

IT WAS three days since Keira had last seen Jay—three days in which she had had time to focus on her work and rebalance her own sense of self.

Where another woman might have found it galling and humiliating to have a man walk away, having started to make love to her, Keira could only feel relieved that Jay had done so. She had been given a second chance to protect herself from her own weakness, and for that she could only be profoundly grateful.

But being grateful wasn't doing anything to ease the ache that had woken her from her sleep last night—and the night before, and the night before that. Keira stared grimly at her laptop screen, battling determinedly to will away such potentially dangerous thoughts. Was this the way her mother had felt about the married man she had once told Keira was her father, whose desertion she claimed had pushed her into the arms of a series of other men?

But then her mother had told her so many different stories, changing with her mood and her need for the drugs on which she'd been dependent. Keira pushed her laptop away from her with an awkward panic-stricken movement that betrayed what she was feeling.

She was not like her mother. She was her own self—an individual who had the power of authority and choice over what she did. No man could make her choose to want him against her will. No man—but what about her own emotions? Emotions? What Jay had aroused within her had nothing to do with emotions. Her desire for him had been sexual, that was all. Nothing more. That was impossible. Just like desiring him in the first place had also been impossible?

Keira's panic increased. She got up and went to the window, but looking down into the courtyard was a mistake. It might be bathed in sunlight now, but inside her head she could still picture it shadowed by moonlight, with Jay's body and her own shadowed along with it. In those shadows they had touched and kissed, and she had—but, no—she must not think of that.

She had an appointment in half an hour, to meet up with the fabric merchant, who had telephoned her to tell her that her samples had arrived. He had offered to bring them to the palace, but Keira had told him that she would go to him.

She had fallen in love with the city, and readily used any excuse to see more of it. She felt so at home here, so at peace—or rather she would have if she hadn't been dreading Jay's return.

The city had been laid out in a geometric grid of streets and squares. From the main square, opposite the palace, a network of narrow pedestrian streets branched out from the straight ceremonial main road that led to the city's main gates, along which in previous centuries the formal processions of maharajas and other dignitaries had passed.

It was these streets, with their stalls and artisan workshops, that fascinated Keira even more than the elegant palaces of the rich. Behind them lay the *bavelis*, the townhouses of the city's original eminent citizens, each of them an individual work of art in its own right.

As always, the rich mingling of scents and sounds absorbed Keira's attention. The sound of temple bells mingled with the laughter of children and the urgent cries of shopkeepers wanting to sell their merchandise.

Knowing she had time in hand, Keira made a detour from her destination that took her past the bazaar, famous for selling rose, almond, saffron and vetiver-flavoured sherbets. In the flower market workers were busy weaving garlands and making floral offerings for templegoers, and when she cut through the jewellery quarter of the bazaar Keira had to force herself not to be tempted to linger outside the shops of the *lac* bangle sellers.

These were the sights and sounds of Jay's home—the place where he had been born, the place where his family had ruled for so many generations. Where his family still ruled. Jay wasn't merely a successful and wealthy entrepreneur, he was also a member of one of India's royal families. His brother was the Maharaja. It was no wonder that he had that air of arrogance and pride about him. No wonder that he believed he could command others to his will.

But it wasn't the command of his royal status that she feared. Rather, it was the command of his essential sensuality—and he would have had that no matter what rank he had been born to, she suspected.

The merchant greeted her with great ceremony, bowing his head so much that Keira momentarily feared for the fate of his ornate turban. His daughter-in-law brought them tea, her sweet, shy smile echoing those of her children. She looked outstandingly pretty in her crimson and blue embroidered *ghaghara* gathered skirt, her *odhni* tucked into the waist of her skirt. She pulled the *odhni* round to drape it modestly over her head, her movements delicate and graceful, her hands and feet carefully patterned with henna.

When Keira saw the fabrics the merchant was spreading out on the floor in front of her she felt her heart skip a beat in delight. She studied the samples that were so excellently in tune with her own ideas, combining as they did tradition with a certain stylish modern twist.

'My cousin would like to invite you to visit his factory, so that you can see more of their work,' the merchant told her.

'Go to his town?' Keira queried excitedly 'Oh, yes. I would love to.'

'My cousin has a new designer, a man from your own country. He would like you to meet him so that you can discuss your requirements with him.'

Before Keira left the shop it was arranged that the merchant would contact his cousin, accepting his invitation on her behalf, whilst Keira would make arrangements via Jay's servants for a car and a driver to be put at her disposal to take her to the fabric town.

If when Jay returned she had proper samples of the fabrics she wanted to use, having consulted directly with the designer and producer, it would surely prove to him that whilst he had been away she had been far too busy working to have any time to waste on thinking about him.

Keira was still desperately trying to convince herself that it was India itself that was responsible for the overwhelming of her defences: India, with its potent mystery and sensuality that thrummed in the air and filled the senses, stealing away reality and resistance. It was India that was responsible for the fact that she lay awake in her bed at night, trying to deny the ache spreading through her in slow waves of heat and need. India that somehow, like a magician, conjured up those unwanted and forbidden images inside her head, created those secret private mental films in which she and Jay lay together, their naked bodies veiled only by the sheer voile bed-hangings enclosing them in their own intimate world.

Yes, it was India that had the power to touch her senses and break through her defences. Not Jay himself, Keira reassured herself.

Mumbai was its normal highly charged cosmopolitan self, Jay acknowledged. With meetings overrunning into cocktail and dinner parties that went on into the early hours of the morning as the socialites of the city mingled with its movers and shakers.

Tonight he was dining with a fellow entrepreneur, an Indian in his early fifties, originally educated in England, who had returned to Mumbai to take over a family business. Amongst the guests was a Bollywood actress who was currently trying to engage Jay's interest in something more intimate than dinner table conversation by asking him if he had yet visited the city's latest exclusive nightclub.

She was very beautiful, with the kind of figure that could make a grown man cry, and her fingertips rested lightly on Jay's suit-clad arm as she leaned closer to him to envelop him in a cloud of scent. Her movements were designed to be sensual and discreetly erotic, but for some reason they failed to stir his pulses. Her scent wasn't the scent he wanted to breathe in, her eyes weren't amber but dark brown, and whilst her touch did nothing whatsoever for him, he only had to think about Keira's touch for his body to react.

What nonsense was this? That one woman could quite easily be replaced by another was Jay's personal mantra—one he adhered to strictly. Jay moved restlessly in his chair, oblivious to the disappointment of his companion as she recognised his lack of interest in her. There was only one explanation he was willing to accept for Keira's unwanted intrusion into his thoughts, and that was quite simply that he ached for her because he had not brought their intimacy to its natural conclusion. If he had done so then he would not still be wanting her. That was all there was to it. Nothing more. Nothing more at all.

Jay was still repeating those words to himself several hours later, as he lay alone and sleepless in his bed in his hotel suite, the business documents he had intended to study left ignored on the beside table.

Keira.

Jay closed his eyes, only realising his mistake when immediately his memory furnished him with a mental image of her in which her eyes burned dark gold with desire for him and her breath came in swift, unsteady little gasps of escalating arousal.

His own heartbeat picked up, hammering its message of need through his body.

He had been a fool not to take what had been on offer. She had probably had condoms to hand—women like her were always prepared.

The Bollywood actress had insisted on writing down her mobile number for him. He had two more days in Mumbai—could spend longer there if he chose. Longer? Since when did it take more than one night in bed with any woman to satisfy his desire for her? Wasn't that why he had grown bored with the ritual of pretending to have to seduce a woman who had already made it plain that she was up for sex with him, taking her shopping for the present she had made it clear she expected, then finding that, like a tiger fed on tame game instead of having to hunt, his belly was full in the sexual sense, but his appetite was somehow not satisfied. It was no wonder that he had actually welcomed the celibacy that had become his only sleeping partner these last few months.

And wasn't it in reality that very celibacy that was responsible for the white heat of his desire for Keira?

Keira. His thoughts had turned full circle, and his body now ached like hell. Jay threw back the bedcovers. Picking up the documents from the bedside table, he strode naked to the desk. He pulled on a robe and switched on his laptop, and proceeded to do what he could to blot Keira out of his thoughts by engrossing himself in some work...

'Oh, I love this toile,' Keira enthused as she studied the fabric sample in front of her, with its design of Indian palaces, monkeys, elephants and howdas printed in traditional single colours against the creamy white of the cotton background.

'I designed it myself,' Alex Jardine told her with a smile. 'I had some original copperplate rollers for toile fabric I was lucky enough to pick up in an antique market in France years ago, and when I showed them to Arjun, here, and explained what I wanted to do, he was able to find me a craftsman to copy the rollers for us so we could create this toile. It's one of four we've been experimenting with: two traditional, of which this is one, and two very contemporary designs.'

Keira nodded her head, fascinated by the designs.

'We're experimenting at the moment with charcoal, to black-dye the modern toile and give it a more edgy look,' he continued.

From the moment she had stepped into the fabric factory Keira had felt as though she had stepped into her own private Aladdin's cave. Bolts of fabrics of every hue imaginable were stacked to the ceiling, mouthwatering acid sherbet colours, rich traditional colours of crimson ruby, jade and emerald embellished with gold thread, sea and sky colours, and even pale creamy naturals. Her senses had fed on them as greedily as a child let loose in a sweet shop, and now she was every bit as giddy and dizzy as that child might have been, from consuming too many additives. She was on a high with the sheer intensity of her own rush of delight. And that delight was compounded by her sense of having met someone so much in tune with her own way of thinking in Alex.

At first sight she had felt slightly put off by him. Over six foot tall, with thick curly hair that reached down to his shoulders, he was dressed in white linen trousers, a loose linen shirt and with his feet bare. His voice was a languid 'okay yah' upper crust London drawl, and Keira had felt initially that there was rather too much of the *faux* hippie about him—so much so, in fact, that it was almost a theatrical affectation.

But then he had shown her his fabrics, his large hands as tender on them as though they were small children, his voice softening as he told her about their provenance and his own desire to keep his designs true to tradition whilst bringing in something unique and modern that was still 'of India', and Keira had been entranced and captivated.

'I am hoping that we'll be able to design something that has a bit of a Bollywood twist to it, but Arjun, here, thinks I'm being over-confident.' Alex laughed as he smiled at the factory owner.

'I just love what you're doing,' Keira told him. 'And if it was up to me I'd be buying up everything for this new venture, but I don't have that authority.'

'We can supply you with samples and you can show them to His Highness Prince Jayesh,' the factory owner was assuring her eagerly.

'Arjun won't let you leave until he's heaped you with samples,' Alex warned her, with a warm smile, reaching out to pluck a stray thread of cotton that had attached itself to the sleeve of her top as the factory owner hurried away for more samples.

Keira smiled back at him, unaware of the fact that Jay had just walked into the building and was standing watching the byplay between them with a glacier cold look in his eyes.

It was Alex who saw Jay first, his own gaze sharpening in recognition of what he could see in Jay's eyes as he strode towards them.

'There's a very angry-looking alpha male heading this way,' he told Keira drolly. 'And he looks very much as though he thinks I've been trespassing on his private property.'

'What?' Puzzled, Keira turned round and then gave a small 'oh' of mixed comprehension and surprise as Jay bore down on them, her stomach churning out its message of acute physical awareness of him as her heart pounded erratically.

He was wearing light linen, apparently oblivious to the heat in the factory, with no sign of perspiration dampening his skin in the way Keira knew it was dampening her own—although she could see the dark shadow along his jaw where he needed to shave. It gave him an extra edge of raw masculinity that touched her own femaleness as directly as though he himself had touched her—very intimately.

A giddy, nerve-tingling feeling had somehow taken hold of her, reminiscent of the way she felt after drinking champagne. Bubbles of sensation fizzed through her veins, heightening her awareness of him and her sensitivity to him. Her gaze was somehow drawn to his face, and refused to be moved. It was as though she had been possessed by the greed of a hedonist with an insatiable appetite, Keira decided shakily, unable to stop herself from visually gorging herself on the pleasure of looking at him.

Jay—here! What an extraordinary coincidence that he should have business here himself. Not that he looked at all pleased to have found her here, she noticed.

'Jay,' she greeted him weakly. 'You've come back early from Mumbai. I'm so glad you're here. I've just seen the most wonderful fabrics. You're going to love them, I know…' She was gabbling like an idiot, unable to stop herself as she plucked sample after sample from the pile Arjun had just returned with, wafting them before Jay's totally immobile gaze.

He hadn't spoken or moved, hadn't so much as acknowledged her in any way, and yet he filled her senses. All she could see, all she knew, was him.

'You must meet Alex,' Keira gabbled on. 'He's got the most wonderful ideas—'

She broke off as she physically felt the increase in tension, as clearly as though someone had actually tightened the air and removed oxygen from it. Jay's lips had thinned, his gaze icing over her before being directed past her to Alex.

'Arjun's got all the samples Keira and I have discussed,' Keira heard Alex saying easily. 'But you'll want to check them out for yourself, and as Keira knows I'm open to whatever input she wants to give me. Next time you come to visit, if you let me know beforehand, Keira, I'll book you into that boutique hotel I was telling you about and we can do dinner,' Alex offered, giving Keira another smile. 'And then I'll have time to show you what I can really do.'

When he winked at her and grinned, Keira couldn't help but laugh. Alex was a tease, but harmless, and she didn't in any way object to his mild social flirting, knowing it for what it was—which was nothing more than something to oil the wheels of business.

She would have liked to stay a bit longer, to share her enthusiasm and excitement for what she had seen with Jay, but he was making it very plain that he was not in the mood to look at fabrics and was clearly waiting to leave. He was also making it very obvious that he was expecting her to leave with him. Presumably he had completed his own business, whatever it had been, and so Keira thanked Arjun and allowed Jay to escort her out of the factory, whilst two young boys carried her precious samples over to the car and handed them to her driver.

However, when Keira made to follow them to her car, Jay stopped her.

'You're travelling back with me,' he told her abruptly.

She could have objected—perhaps she should have objected, given his dictatorial manner—but for some reason she remained strangely silent. Not because she actually wanted to travel back with him, of course, Keira insisted to herself as Jay opened the passenger door of his Mercedes and then stood beside it, waiting for her to get inside more in the manner of a gaoler than anything else. Keira winced when he closed the door with a definite thud.

It was late in the day and the town was busy with traffic, filling its narrow streets. All too conscious of the hazards presented by small children darting out into the road, plus old people, cyclists, bullock carts, the highly decorated trucks that were so much a part of India's road culture, not to mention stray cows and other cars, Keira didn't venture to speak for fear of distracting Jay's attention from his driving.

Once clear of the town, though, when Jay himself made no attempt to engage her in conversation, Keira found that despite the oppressive atmosphere caused by his silence she didn't feel brave enough to break it.

With the sun setting over the dusty plain she focused instead on the view beyond the window, and she couldn't stop herself from exclaiming aloud in delight when they passed a herd of camels being made ready to travel as they took advantage of the evening coolness.

'We're so close to the desert that I'd love to take the opportunity to see the annual Cattle Fair,' she told Jay enthusiastically. 'Have you seen it?' she asked him.

'Of course,' Jay told her shortly.

Of course he would have. This was his country, after all, Keira reminded herself. His manner was so European that she tended to forget that at times.

It made her feel uncomfortable and on edge to recognise that just the fact of seeing Jay when she hadn't expected to do so had had such a dramatic effect on her mood, changing her from an in-control businesswoman into someone whose every reaction was controlled by her awareness of him: a smile from him sent her heart soaring upwards, and a frown had it plunging downwards.

No one had affected her like this before, and knowing that he could and did made her feel on edge and vulnerable. She wanted to reject completely the pull he had on her senses, and yet at the same time she was drawn helplessly to check over and over again the intensity of it—like a moth drawn to the light that would ultimately destroy it, she thought with a small shiver, witnessing the helpless suicide of the soft-winged creatures as they flew into the beam of the car's headlights, switched on now that darkness had fallen.

The lights of the city broke the stark emptiness of the plain as they drove closer to it.

Jay was still struggling within himself to justify his intense and uncharacteristic reaction to the fact that Keira had been absent from the palace on his return.

That he had automatically expected she would be there and had been so infuriated when she was not had been bad enough, but he might have dismissed those feelings as being caused by the ongoing sexual challenge she represented to him. However, explaining his own sense of aloneness and the emptiness of the building without her in it was something else again, and something for which he could not find any logical reason.

In short, it had infuriated him to return and find her gone. It had infuriated him even more to have to admit to his own reaction to her absence. And it had infuriated him most of all to have to endure his own inner sense of desolation and the emptiness of the palace without her.

Why on earth should the absence of one woman—a woman he barely knew—affect him to such an extent that he had been driven to set out in pursuit of her? It was simply not logical. And it was most definitely not acceptable.

Jay considered himself to be a man who had overcome the human weakness of being held hostage to emotion. Everything he did was governed and motivated by reason and rationality. Of course he permitted himself to be pleased when his goals and objectives were achieved, but it was a controlled and disciplined satisfaction. Not for Jay the pantomiming, posturing foolishness of the type who found it necessary to trumpet their success to the world in ridiculous displays of conspicuous consumption, which invariably involved magnums of champagne, flashy models and equally flashy so-called 'boys' toys'.

Yes, he *had* celebrated his successes—with a carefully chosen piece of art, or an addition to his worldwide property portfolio, and always a generous anonymous donation to those charities he supported. These were charities in the main that provided for orphaned children in the poorest of the world's countries, but this was a private matters.

What he had experienced today came dangerously close to challenging everything he believed about himself. That must not be allowed to happen. The enormity of what it might mean was too much. It wasn't the intimacy he had witnessed between Keira and her fellow countryman that had affected him. Rather it was his anger at her behaviour and the effect it might have on his own business reputation. Indians placed a great deal of importance on good moral behaviour, and he had no wish to see the reputation of his business tarnished by Keira's flirtatious and unprofessional manner. *That* was the cause of his anger, and it was perfectly logical. It had nothing whatsoever to do with emotion—and certainly not an emotion like jealousy.

They had reached the palace car park. Without a word to Keira Jay stopped the car, got out, and then went round to open the passenger door for her.

They were back inside the palace before Keira could find the courage to break the crushing silence Jay had imposed, telling him brightly, 'I'd better go and thank my driver, and retrieve the samples...'

'Wait,' Jay demanded curtly. 'There's something I wish to discuss with you first. We'll go to my office,' he told her, gesturing towards the stairs.

Whatever he wanted to say to her it wasn't going to be something she wanted to hear, Keira recognised as she took in the grim set of his mouth and the way he distanced himself from her as they walked up the stairs.

Once they were inside his office Jay closed the door with the same controlled ferocity with which he had closed the car door earlier, the small but definite thud of that closure causing Keira's heart to jolt uneasily into her ribs.

Keira could sense that a storm was brewing as clearly as though she had seen thunderclouds building up and growling ominously on the horizon. It swept into the room without warning or ceremony, feeding on the oxygen in the air and leaving her chest tight as she struggled to breathe in the air that was left.

When Jay spoke, his words were like sheet lightning, slicing through the stifling silence.

'You had no business travelling so far out of

the city without advising me of your plans beforehand.'

'You weren't here, and—'

'And you couldn't wait?' Jay challenged her coldly.

Keira gulped in air, bewildered by his anger.

'You were the one who introduced me to the fabric merchant so that I could obtain some samples,' she reminded him.

'The merchant, yes. But I most certainly did not suggest that you, a woman on your own, should travel anywhere unescorted, and that once having done so—'

'I was not unescorted,' Keira protested. 'I was with my driver. I'd gone there on business to—'

'To flirt with one of your own countrymen?'

'No!'

'Yes. Since that is most certainly what you were doing when I saw you.'

'What? That's ridiculous,' Keira defended herself.

'But you knew that he would be there?' Jay queried.

'Well, yes,' Keira admitted. 'But—'

'And immediately you knew that, you decided to go and check him out?'

'No! This is crazy. It was the fabric merchant who suggested that I might want to meet the designer and see his work at first hand.'

'Was it? Or did you suggest it yourself? Was it his work you wanted to inspect at first hand or the man himself? A fellow European...'

What he was insinuating was as insulting as it was incorrect, Keira thought angrily.

'I went to check out fabric—Indian fabric. Not a European man, or indeed any kind of man,' Keira told him fiercely. 'I'm not interested in checking out men.'

Too late she realised her mistake. The look Jay slanted her was as steely sharp as a new blade.

'No? That's not the impression you've been giving me,' he taunted her.

Another minute and he'd be reminding her of her response to him. Keira tensed herself inwardly for the expected verbal blow, but to her relief instead he accused her coldly.

'You were flirting with him—you can't deny that.'

Relief washed through her, chilling the heat of her earlier anger.

'Yes, I can—and I do.'

Ignoring her protest, Jay insisted grimly, 'Admit it. You were coming on to him so hard that you were oblivious to anyone and everything else—not that he was objecting. He was as eager to get you into his bed as you were to be there. That was patently obvious.'

'That is *not* true, and I was *not* coming on to him,' Keira denied truthfully again. 'We were simply both being polite to one another.' She was getting her courage back now that she had escaped the humiliation of him reminding her how passionately she responded to him. 'Good manners are a highly valued trait in Indian society—something that Indian children are taught at their mother's knee. As I should have thought you would know.'

The silence was suddenly alive with the kind of danger that brought up the small hairs on the back of her neck.

'So you maintain that you were simply being polite, do you?'

'Yes,' Keira insisted.

'By offering yourself to him?'

'I was *not* doing that.'

'Yes, you were. Just like you've been offering yourself to me from the first moment we met.'

'That's not true!' Keira had had enough. She had to get out of this room and away from this man.

Shaking her head, she made for the door—only Jay got there ahead of her, barring her way with his body so that she virtually ran full-tilt into him.

She could feel the heat of his breath on her skin and the bite of his fingers into her upper arms. Her only means of escape was to close her eyes and try desperately to shut down her senses. But it was too late. Jay was swinging her round to imprison her against the wall, his mouth plundering hers. It was pointless trying to resist when her own body was in revolt and had turned traitor on her, joining Jay instead and offering itself up to him.

How could she want such an emotionally humiliating intimacy? How could she not reject the hot pouring tide of a sensuality she knew to be corrupted with the poison of contempt and lust? How could she moan and soften within the hardness of Jay's hold, seeking to give all of herself up to him?

She didn't know. But then she was past knowing anything other than the intensity of her need for Jay.

Her own arms were wrapped tightly around him now, her breasts sensitised by the movement of her body against his. Inside her head she could already see his hands covering their nakedness, feel the fierce tug of his mouth against her nipples.

She shuddered violently in reaction to her own thoughts. A sharp spike of shock pierced through her, only to be overwhelmed by a fresh wave of aching longing as Jay pressed her even more closely to him, his hands moving up over her body to her breasts, cupping them urging them, free of their covering. Lamplight stroked the pale alabaster of her skin, latticed with the darker shadows of Jay's hands, and her nipples were desire-engorged and tight as she pressed into the cup of his palms. Just the simple act of his palms brushing against their tenderness was enough to make Keira shudder with need.

She couldn't bear there to be any barriers between them. She wanted his hands on her body. She wanted the freedom to explore and caress his body. She wanted to touch and taste him, know him and know his knowing of her, his full possession of her. Those feelings were like a form of madness in her blood that she couldn't withstand. They filled her head with images of them together and turned her body into an aching mass of yearning nerve-endings and willing flesh, created only for this man and this moment.

He felt hard and erect, ready for her in the same openly sexual way in which she knew her own body was ready for him. She could feel the damp softness between her legs, and the quick fierce pulse that went with it. She wanted desperately for him to touch her there, for him to caress her there. A small moan bubbled in her throat, followed by a shuddering gasp in acknowledgement of his accuracy in reading her mind when his hand dropped from her breast to her belly and then slid lower over her thigh, beneath her skirt, his fingers probing the edge of her thin silky knickers.

His kiss matched the intimate possession of his fingers. The very fact that the deliberate thrust of his tongue was more demanding than the delicate questing of the fingertip he rubbed against the wetness of her clitoris told her more clearly than any words that he was holding back—just as her own shudder of response and acceptance told him that she was eager to answer that demand.

But instead of taking things further Jay's mouth left hers, to move slowly along her jaw and towards her ear.

Keira didn't know which she wanted most… what he was doing or what he had been doing. Just the whisper of his breath…his lips against her skin…was sending her crazy.

Not that he was exactly immune to the reaction he was arousing in her either, by the way he was gripping her hips and pulling her tightly against his body, Keira recognised, with a fierce thrill of female pleasure.

Now it was her turn to groan aloud with delight as his hand moved back up her body and cupped her breast. Just the feel of his thumb tip rubbing sensuously across her tight aching nipple made her moan out loud.

She had to bite on her bottom lip to stop herself from begging him to take off her top and expose her breast to his gaze, his touch, to the hot hard caress of his mouth.

Frantically she tensed her muscles, squeezing her thighs together as she felt a surge of longing rocket through her.

As though he guessed what was happening to her Jay cupped her hip, his fingers kneading her rhythmically. She was leaning fully against the wall now, whilst Jay's hands caressed every inch of her, making her quiver from head to foot in open longing.

Was this something he had learned from the *Kama Sutra*?

When he took her hand and placed it against

his own body she almost sobbed with pleasure. Her hands were long and slender, but the hard swollen length of him extended beyond her outstretched fingertips. Keira closed her eyes, pleasure a dark velvet blanket of sensuality behind her closed eyelids. She ached as though she had a fever for the feel of him inside her. She had had no idea there could be desire like this—instant, immediate, hot and hungry, a need that burned everything else into oblivion and drove a person on relentlessly until it was sated.

No doubt if Jay knew the truth about her he would think her very unworldly not to have experienced something like this before. Unlike him!

How many times…? How many women…? That thought burned through her in a hot agony of molten jealousy that stabbed through her, stiffening her body into rigid rejection of what she was feeling and thinking.

Abruptly she was shocked back into reality, her desire chilling into sick self-disgust. What was she thinking of? How could she be behaving like this when she knew…?

Panic twisted and speared inside her.

She had to get away from him—now. Before it was too late and she became one of those women, a woman like her mother, who loved the wrong man and made the wrong choices.

Loved…

Keira started to tremble violently with reaction. Jay's hands were still on her body but she pushed them away, taking him by surprise and opening the door before he could stop her.

Once free of his office she started to walk faster, finally breaking into a run so that by the time she had reached the sanctuary of her room her heart was thudding against her chest wall. From exertion, or from the fear she had brought from Jay's office with her? The fear that she might be falling in love with him.

Keira sank down onto her bed, her head in her hands.

Jay could feel beads of sweat forming on his skin and then chilling as he fought to regain his self-control. He could hear the sound of his own breathing, shallow and strained, whilst his heart thudded and pounded accusingly against his ribs. His body ached and raged against its denial, but Jay was more concerned with his inability to control his emotions rather than any inability to control his flesh.

How could it have happened? How could he have allowed his physical desire for a woman to lead him into the kind of behaviour he had exhibited today? Pursuing her, burning up with fury because he had seen her smiling at another man, wanting to physically stamp his possession on her and deny that same opportunity to any other man.

Jay strode across the room and threw open the shutters to let in the night air. But nothing could rid his senses of the scent of Keira, and of his own arousal. They clung together, wrapped around one another as though they belonged together, filling his head with tormenting images. How *could* they belong together?

Sex was an act that took place between two separate people who returned to that separateness. If Keira hadn't run from him he would have taken her to bed...

But she had, ignoring both her own arousal and his. And she *had* been aroused. Jay knew that. He moved awkwardly, forced to tense his body against the still far too potent memory of how she had reacted when he had touched her, her lips clinging to his, her nipples swelling tightly into his palm, her sex soft and wet.

Irritably Jay speedily shut down the too easily conjured up mental pleasure his senses were giving him. He was a fool if he couldn't recognise that a good part of the reason he wanted her was the fact that she was playing a game that meant he couldn't have her. A game in which she offered and then withdrew that offer. A game that was one of the oldest in the world.

He took a deep breath of the cool air. It was totally illogical that he should continue to want her, knowing what she was. But a feeling he didn't want to admit to twisted his belly. Jealousy? Savagely he dismissed the mocking inner voice he didn't want to hear. It was impossible for him to feel jealous. Jealousy was an emotion, and he simply did not 'do' emotions. Not ever—not with anyone.

If he had any sense he would terminate her contract immediately and send her back to England with a compensation payment. He would negotiate with her to buy her designs and put a new team in place to put them into practice. That way if, by some impossible to imagine chance, he *had* somehow become vulnerable to some kind of hitherto never experienced male folly, then it would be brought to a swift end.

Yes, that was what he must do. Just as soon as he got back from Mumbai.

CHAPTER EIGHT

HER head on one side, Keira carefully studied the newly painted walls of the show house. She had chosen the paint from over a dozen different samples, all of which had been applied in square patches to the wall so that she could assess the effect on the room's light and size.

'Yes,' she told the waiting painter with a pleased smile. 'That's perfect.'

Someone else might not consider it worthwhile on such a tight schedule to spend time finding exactly the right shade of off-white, but to Keira such niceties were an essential part of the way she worked. The right paint would provide the foundations of her scheme, and thus in her opinion was vitally important. Combining both Jay's wishes and Alex's advice, she had sourced her paint locally, and the supplier had been marvellously patient about fine-tuning the pigment to get the shade she wanted.

The painter was smiling broadly himself now, a huge watermelon grin stretching across his face as he promised her that he would have the paint mixed and delivered to her ready for the decorators to start work in the morning.

It was a month since the evening she had fled—not just from Jay, but more tellingly from her own response to him—to spend virtually the whole night curled up on her bed, agonising over what she should do.

The discovery in the morning that Jay had returned to Mumbai had given her a breathing space that had enabled her to think logically and practically about her situation and her options. She had reasoned that financially she could not afford to break her contract, whilst emotionally and sexually she could not afford to mirror her mother's folly in falling in love with the wrong man and going to bed with him.

Jay inhabited a world in which the super-rich called nowhere home. It was unlikely that their paths would ever cross again once she had finished her work here. Reasonably, therefore, all she had to do was keep her distance from him until life put an even greater distance between them. Once it had she could ache all she wanted for him, in the secure knowledge that all she *could* do was ache. Better to burn with unappeased longing than to be destroyed be the acid corrosion of shame and self-disgust.

And anyway, now she was alert to her own danger she had herself properly under control, Keira assured herself firmly.

Really? So why, then, was her stomach now twisting itself in knots just because she could see Jay walking towards her?

He was here, and her world had tilted on its axis. But she could act naturally and keep things on a professional footing, Keira decided, and she told him briskly, 'Jamil has been very patient with me, and we've finally got the right paint colour. The decorators should be able to start work tomorrow, and by the time they've finished the furniture and soft furnishings should be starting to arrive.'

Jay nodded his head.

'You haven't given me a decision yet on the toile fabric I discussed with you,' Keira reminded him. 'So if you've got time…'

'You mean your fellow countryman's designs?' Jay stopped her.

'Yes,' Keira agreed, telling him enthusiastically, 'I thought his contemporary designs were fun and quirky and would appeal to buyers—especially if we move away from the traditional French colours into something more dramatic and modern. Black on hot pink or bright yellow would make a real statement if we used it on cushions, for instance.'

'And of course if I agree to buy your countryman's designs then naturally he's going to want to show his gratitude—probably in a private suite at that hotel he was discussing with you.' The sardonic tone of Jay's voice coupled with the innuendo of his words made Keira's heart plummet downwards.

'That is grossly unfair and insulting,' she told him furiously. 'There is only one reason I would ever recommend anyone to a client, and that is because, in my professional opinion, they or their product are right for the job. That is the way I do business. You, of course, may have other methods.'

'You *dare* to accuse me of your own low moral standards?'

Jay looked so angry as he took a step towards her and stood almost menacingly over her, filling the air with the heat of his fury, that Keira wasn't sure what would have happened if the site manager hadn't come and interrupted them, explaining that there were some papers he needed Jay to sign.

The sooner this commission was completed and she could end her association with Jay the better, Keira told herself fiercely.

She had an appointment to meet with one of the manufacturers who was providing some of the furniture for the show homes tomorrow. His factory was several hours' drive away, in a small town close to the border of the desert. Remembering what had happened when she had gone to visit the fabric factory, this time Keira had sent a message first to Jay, explaining what she intended to do and requesting his approval. He had not said anything about it just now.

Keira's heart slid heavily into her ribs. It was no use trying to lie to herself. Each time she saw him she might promise herself that this time she would not permit herself to endure that surge of sick, aching need that made her long to be in his arms even though she knew that that was the worst place she could ever be, but she knew that in reality it was a promise she would never be able to keep.

Take today. It was just over four weeks since she had last seen him—four weeks, two days and ten minutes, to be exact. Well, twenty minutes if she counted the extra ten minutes she had spent concealed behind the fretwork of the latticed *jails,* designed to keep the women of the harem from public view whilst enabling them to look down into the street below, watching Jay walk away from the palace.

Four weeks during which she had resolutely focused on her work, filling every heartbeat of time with a feverish busyness designed to deny her the ability to give in to the temptation to think about Jay. She had even taken to reading books on Indian culture and crafts when she went to bed, until her eyes became too heavy to stay open.

And yet earlier today, the minute she had looked up and seen him, every rule she had made to protect herself had been ignored and forgotten.

It had taken his insulting remark about Alex to force her to recognise reality.

In that regard at least she was most certainly not her mother's daughter, Keira recognised tiredly. She felt no quickening of her senses at all where other men were concerned.

Which made her danger greater rather than less. Loving the wrong man could be every bit as destructive as loving too many wrong men—especially when that wrong man was a man like Jay.

Jay leaned against one of the pillars supporting the vaulted ceiling of the palace's main reception room. The walls and the pillars were decorated with a traditional form of plasterwork that had been hand polished with a piece of agate, to create a marble finish, but of course that finish was a fake, false—just like Keira. Did she really think he had been deceived by that protest of hers about her fabric designer friend?

Jay paced the room restlessly. He had gone to Mumbai to escape from the ache of wanting her that being here with her gave him. He had even sworn that he would ease that ache in the arms of the actress who had been so delighted to hear from him. So why hadn't he done exactly that? And why had he cut short his visit and returned here ahead of schedule?

He wasn't going to answer that question. Why should he, when he had so many far more important matters to concern himself with?

Keira's heart sank as she stood in the main entrance hall to the palace. Her driver had just brought her the unwelcome news that he was not going to be driving her to her appointment but that instead Jay was going to take her, and that he would join her shortly.

Up above her was the gallery she had just walked along, which separated the main part of the palace from the women's quarters, where once they had lived in Purdah.

Purdah! The concealment of a woman's face and body from the eyes of all men except those of her immediate family. To some a protection, but to others a form of imprisonment. As a Western woman the very thought of enduring Purdah was beyond comprehension.

But wasn't the reality that what she herself was enduring, and had endured for most of her life, was in its own way an inner form of Purdah, imposed on her by her own fears? Her Purdah meant that her emotions and desires must always remain hidden away, denied the light of day for her own protection.

Keira tensed as she heard Jay's now familiar footsteps crossing the hallway.

'I'm sorry to have kept you waiting.'

How formal he sounded—and looked, Keira thought, contrasting his immaculate appearance in a perfectly fitting lightweight neutral-coloured suit worn over a pale blue shirt with her own jeans and shirt. But then she had dressed for the bumpy, dusty ride she had been anticipating. Her driver tended to keep the windows of the car open rather than use the air-conditioning, so that he could engage in conversation with other drivers.

They were in the car before Jay spoke to her again.

'Remind me again what the purpose of your visit to this manufacturer is?'

The sarcastic tone of his voice made Keira wish even more that he had not chosen to accompany her.

'I want to see the finished furniture before it is delivered, to make sure that it will work. He's making some special shelving units for the larger properties. They're to go into the studies and the children's rooms, and I wanted to see how he's getting on with them. If my idea works I thought they could be adapted to various age groups if they were given different paint finishes. I also wanted to make sure that he understands that all the paint used must be lead-free. I'm trying where possible to ensure that all the raw materials used come from sustainable sources. Green issues are just as big here in

India with the middle classes as they are in Europe, of course.'

Jay had been driving fast, but now he had slowed down to allow for the leisurely progress of several camel carts.

'I see. And can I be confident that this designer is not another of your countrymen, looking for what you are so obviously eager to give?'

He was hateful, horrible, making accusations without any justification to back them up. Except that in his arms she *had* been eager to give, hadn't she? And she could hardly tell him that he was the first, the last and the only man to whom she had wanted to give herself. Even if she did he wouldn't believe her, and if he ever got to know about her background and her mother, he'd think he had even more reason for his accusations.

'I am not the one who controls what you do or don't think,' was the only thing she could think of to say to him to show her feelings about his comment.

But it was no use. He swooped on her words

as swiftly as a predatory bird of prey to the lure—so much so, in fact, that she could almost feel the verbal bite of his sharp talons as he countered, 'But you are the one whose behaviour gives rise to my thoughts.'

Keira had had enough.

'If you choose to think that a simple light-hearted exchange of words between a man and a woman is tantamount to an offer of sex then I feel sorry for you—or rather I feel sorry for the women who are the victims of your prejudice, should they happen to indulge in what they think is lighthearted conversation with you.'

'Your sex does not indulge in lighthearted conversation. It plans the course of its words with military precision—from the minute a woman makes an approach to a man to the minute he hands over to her the reward she has already decided he will give her in exchange for the pleasure of her company.'

'That is just cynical and unfair. There may be some women who do do that, but—'

'Some women—of which you are one, as we both already know.'

Keira knew there was nothing she could say that would make him accept that he was wrong about her. And why should she care if he did? What benefit would it be to her? It would simply make her even more vulnerable to him. At least this way she had his contempt of her to strengthen her determination not to allow her feelings for him to betray her.

The furniture factory was outside a small, dusty and very busy town on the caravan route where the plain met the desert.

Henna painters sat cross-legged on the roadside, hoping for passing custom; up ahead of them a farmer was unloading cackling chickens onto a stall ready to sell, whilst hot food was already on sale at another stall, filling the air with the scent of spices and cinnamon. A group of temple musicians walked past, their brightly coloured turbans contrasting with their white clothes.

'The factory is over there,' she told Jay, pointing in the direction of a two-storey building set apart from the others.

The desert heat hit Keira the minute she stepped out of the air-conditioned car. It was post-monsoon now, and she couldn't imagine what it must be like in the oppressive heat before the rains came.

The air was sharp with the smell of glue and paint, stinging her nostrils and making her catch her breath.

Their arrival had obviously been noticed, because the door to the factory owner's office had opened and the owner himself was hurrying towards them. Keira saw the anxious look he gave Jay, and felt sorry for him. Jay was an extraordinarily formidable man, especially when his mouth was compressed and he was frowning, as he was doing now.

'Hello, Mr Singh,' Keira greeted the factory owner. 'Please let me introduce His Highness Prince Jayesh to you.'

Keira could see how awed the factory owner was by Jay—which was hardly surprising. Jay dwarfed the other man, physically and materially, and poor Mr Singh was looking more anxious by the second.

They were ushered towards the office with many bows and a great deal of ceremony. The factory owner was plainly on edge, but no more than Keira was herself. This was a big test of her ability not just to locate and order furniture, but also to ensure that what she had ordered worked with the whole scheme.

She sensed that Jay had accompanied her not just to check up on her, but in the hope that she might fail—and that, of course, added to her anxiety.

'And now, Miss, if you will come, please, and see your shelves?' Mr Singh invited once they had gone through the formality of drinking tea.

Mr Singh led them into an anteroom of the factory, where Keira's shelving had been put on display.

To her relief it was exactly what she had wanted: constructed in sections so that it could be put together in different combinations, to cover an entire wall or merely part of it, either low or high on the wall. These particular shelves had been painted black and then rubbed down for a modern look.

Keira went up to them to inspect them properly, checking the quality of the paintwork and then testing the shelves themselves for stability.

'They are good, yes?' the factory owner asked eagerly.

'Yes,' Keira confirmed.

The factory owner's mobile phone rang. As he turned aside to answer it Keira ran her hand along the underside of one of the shelves, wincing when her finger was pierced by a small splinter of wood and quickly withdrawing her hand to inspect the damage.

'Let me see,' Jay demanded peremptorily

The factory owner had excused himself to deal with his call, and suddenly the small room felt very claustrophobic now that she was alone in it with Jay.

'It's only a splinter,' Keira told him. But he was ignoring her, reaching for her hand and taking hold of it before she could stop him whilst he frowned over the splinter and then expertly removed it.

A single small drop of bright red blood had formed at the exit to the wound, but Keira barely noticed it. All her attention was concentrated on the fact that Jay's fingers were still curled around her wrist, and that he was standing close enough to her for her to hear the sound of his heartbeat.

Her own heartbeat increased in speed. The drop of blood quivered in response to it. Jay looked down at it, and then lifted her hand to his mouth.

Keira drew in a sharp breath and then discovered that she couldn't release it. She started to tremble.

The slow curl of Jay's tongue around her finger felt like rough velvet stroking her skin. Molten heat invaded her body. She wanted to close her eyes and stay with him, savouring this feeling for ever. She wanted... The sound of footsteps outside the door as the factory owner returned jerked her back to reality. She pulled her hand free and exhaled unsteadily.

The factory owner was saying something, but she couldn't concentrate, so it was Jay who responded to him.

How could something so simple be responsible for the sensations and emotions tearing her apart?

CHAPTER NINE

THEY were just over halfway back to the city when Keira happened to glance in the passenger-side wing mirror and notice the stormclouds that were rapidly darkening the sky behind them, piling on top of one another in a leaden grey and densely packed mass.

Jay had obviously seen them too, because he depressed the accelerator and told her crisply, 'Looks like we could be in for a downpour.'

'I thought the monsoon season was over,' Keira told him. The clouds were toppling over one another now, spilling out to cover the sky in a billowing rolling wall that was moving speedily towards them.

'It is,' Jay agreed. 'This is obviously a freak storm of some sort. It can happen. Hold on,' he warned her, as he pressed the accelerator even further and the car surged forward at a speed that sent them bouncing over the poor-quality road.

'I wouldn't normally want to travel at this speed on a road like this, but I'd rather not be caught out here in the open if the storm catches up with us. If a deluge starts this road could all too easily be turned into a river.'

Keira nodded her head, recognising the truth of what he was saying.

The sky was almost purple-black behind them now, and the branches of the scrubby sparse trees were bending and twisting in the ferocity of the wind that was pushing the storm towards them. Flocks of birds rose from the trees, wheeling and screeching before turning to flee. Eerily electric yellow-white lightning flashed behind them, followed by crashes of thunder that made Keira wince and cling to her seat.

She no longer wanted to look in the wing mirror, but of course she couldn't stop herself from doing so. The storm was catching up with them.

'Watch out.'

Jay swung the car to avoid hitting a cow that

had strayed into the road, throwing Keira hard against both her seat belt and the arm he had flung across to protect her. Her own immediate instinct was to hold tightly to his arm, as much for comfort as anything else.

'Sorry about that.'

His voice was clipped, and Keira could feel him tensing his arm, ready to pull away from her as though he was keen to break their physical contact. Just as she should be.

'I'm just glad you managed to avoid the cow,' Keira told him shakily, trying to make some effort at normal conversation to distract herself from the dangerous direction of her thoughts. She released him, and then had to fight not to grab hold of him again as another bolt of lightning lit up the bruised tungsten-dark sky.

Large fat drops of rain hammered down on the car's roof and hit the windscreen, mingling with the dust to turn it into muddy rivulets.

'I'm going to have to slow down,' Jay warned her. 'Otherwise we'll risk aquaplaning off the road.'

Keira nodded her head. She was grateful to

him for keeping her informed of what he was doing and why, but she didn't want to distract him from his driving by talking to him.

Not that she could talk to him now and be heard—not over the noise of the thunder and the rain that was engulfing them.

Sheet lightning illuminated a torrent of rain so powerful that it was as though they were driving under a waterfall. In the car's headlights Keira could see the muddy froth of boiling water where the road used to be.

Jay had cut the car's speed, but Keira could still feel the dangerous suck and pull of the flooding water as it seethed beneath their tyres, threatening to wash them off the road.

Strangely, she didn't feel as afraid as she knew she should. Because she was with Jay? Keira glanced briefly towards him. He was staring ahead, concentrating on his driving, his hands on the steering wheel careful and controlled rather than white-knuckled with anxiety. Somehow she knew that Jay would not let the storm beat him.

'Ralapur's up ahead,' Jay told her, and sure

enough, as Keira peered through the windscreen, she could see here and there the glimmer of lights.

Jay picked up speed again, leaving the storm behind, and they came to the new Tarmac road—commissioned and paid for, she had learned, by Jay's brother, who was proving to be a forward-thinking and caring figurehead. The Tarmac gleamed wet under the drum of the rain, but at least it was free of any surface water.

By the time they reached the city car park the rain had actually almost stopped, but the storm was obviously following them.

'If you want to stay here whilst I go and get you a raincoat and an umbrella—?' Jay offered, as he switched off the engine.

Keira shook her head. 'No, I'll come with you,' she told him. She'd rather risk getting a bit wet and having the safety of his presence than remaining dry and staying in the car on her own.

'Come on, then.'

They were only yards from the square in front of the palace when the storm caught up with them, drenching them with a deluge of rainfall that soaked them through to the skin, hammering down so hard that Keira felt as though she could hardly breathe.

When Jay took hold of her hand, shouting to her above the noise of the rain, 'We'll go this way—it's quicker!' as he half-pulled her down a narrow passageway and through a high gate in the wall that took them into his own private courtyard, she didn't have the breath to object, even if she had wanted to do so. Far easier and safer to simply let Jay lead her up the flight of stone stairs that led from his courtyard to his door, which he opened speedily, pushing Keira inside ahead of him, and then slammed closed behind them, enclosing them both in the welcome dry protection of the room beyond it.

The thought occurred to Keira that not once during the storm had she felt anything less than complete faith in Jay, and complete trust in his judgement as he had made decisions she knew she would not have had the confidence to make. But what she would remember most of all about the storm was the warmth of his hand holding hers. It was pointless telling herself that the sense of intimacy she had felt and the joy it had brought her were completely out of proportion to his actions, and therefore a warning sign of how dangerously out of her depth she was getting. It was too late. She suspected that somehow, somewhere along the journey from their first meeting to being here in this room, she had fallen in love with him.

Out of breath and soaking wet, Keira pushed her realisation aside and looked round the room. A bedroom. Jay's bedroom? Her heart lurched and crashed into her ribs—and not out of fear, she recognized, as Jay strode across the room to switch on the lights.

She was shivering now, and not just because of her body's reaction to the intimacy of their surroundings. Her wet clothes were plastered to her body, just as Jay's were plastered to his. Jay's shirt was clinging to his torso, so sodden that it had become virtually opaque. Her heart was skittering around inside her ribcage now, her mouth was dry and a dangerous and unwanted pulse was aching deep inside her.

Keira dragged her gaze away from its hungry focus on Jay and made herself study her surroundings instead.

A large modern bed dominated the room, with crisp white bedlinen turned down over a richly embroidered silk coverlet. Art Deco lamps with Tiffany shades threw soft shadows across the dark silk-rug-covered floor, repeating the 1930s theme of the women's quarters and reminding Keira that it had been a habit of the fabulously wealthy Maharajas of that era to build themselves new palaces, decorated and furnished in the fashion of the times.

Outside the sky had turned dark, and the only sound was that of the rain hammering down. Keira lifted her hand to brush her wet hair out of her eyes and then nearly jumped out of her skin as suddenly there was a flash of lightning so intense it seared the sky, followed almost immediately by the most deafening crash of thunder. As she cried out, more in shock than fear, the lights went out, plunging the room and the city beyond it into darkness.

Keira took a step forward and then came to an

abrupt halt as she collided with Jay. His fingers curled round her upper arms—to steady her or to hold her off? She didn't know. All she did know was that the mere act of him touching her was setting off a storm of its own inside her body that she knew she would not be able to contain. Desire zig-zagged through her like the lightning outside, burning from nerve-ending to nerve-ending, leaving her a mass of aching, volatile need. Her heart crashed into her ribs. The threat of her longing was causing her far more fear than what was happening outside. Instinctively and immediately Keira tried to protect herself, but it was too late. Her body had other ideas. As she had done before she leaned towards him, the stifled urgent sound of her breathing tattooing onto the silence a sensuality that spoke openly of her desire.

Jay heard the message and recognised it. He should turn her down. But in the electric tension of the darkened room her quickened breathing was suddenly a conduit for the desire he had been fighting to keep at bay from the moment he had first seen her. It ran like fire over gunpowder along his veins and through his senses, blowing apart his control over not just his reactions, but over something he had thought no woman could ever influence—his emotions.

Rejection burned into need; need—that was all, Jay told himself fiercely. The feeling growing within him that she had some kind of unique magnetic pull on his senses was just his imagination.

Ignoring the warnings his brain was trying to give him, he reached for Keira, demanding softly, 'What is it? What do you want? Tell me.'

The ragged catch in her breath quickened his own arousal. He could feel her trembling, smell the scent of her skin, hear the ache in her low moan of longing.

'Is it this?'

He had drawn her to him with one strong, sinuous movement that brought her up tightly against his body.

'Tell me,' he repeated. 'Tell me that you want me.'

This was madness—a madness she would regret. Yet somehow she no longer cared.

'I want you,' Keira whispered. And as though the admission had released her from all constraint, she could feel the wild, wanton rush of her own hot desire as it stormed through her body, overpowering everything that stood in its way. 'I want you,' she repeated unsteadily, but more loudly. 'I want you…'

'How? How do you want me? Tell me. Show me. Show me your desire. Show me the way you want me to please you. Talk to me in words and tell me your pleasure.'

What he was asking of her was impossible, but that didn't stop his words from exciting her almost unbearably.

Their bodies gave off a mutual heat of need through the wet fabric of their clothes. She could smell it, feel it, and breathing it in was like breathing in something headily intoxicating.

Thunder roared overhead, and lightning spat and forked— and Keira's heartbeat went into overdrive.

She registered the rise and fall of Jay's chest with a small shuddering breath. In the dim light his eyes shone molten like mercury, his gaze quicksilver, loaded with promise and danger.

The hot, almost feral scent of Jay's arousal mingling with that of his skin charged a feeling within her so sharp it was almost a pain, and longing leached from her blood into her flesh.

She should not be feeling like this, but it was too late to tell herself that now.

She was torn between her longing for him and her fear because she did so; torn between arousal and animosity, between the intensity of her need to drive him over the edge that would result in him possessing her and the equal intensity of her need to escape from that darkness within herself.

Almost as though he sensed the battle taking place inside her, Jay tightened his hold on her, warning her without words that it was too late now for her to try to escape.

Keira shivered and made a small sound of protest against her own arousal, whispering, 'No…'

'*Yes.*' Jay overruled her. 'Yes.'

His mouth was explosively demanding on her

own, but Keira didn't care. His passion was overwhelming her half-hearted attempt at dutiful resistance, and she was more than glad to let it. She had to respond to him. There was no other choice, and nor did she wish for one. This was what she had been yearning and aching for. This was what she had been born for.

The storm had engulfed them both, and Keira was swamped by it. In the warm darkness of the room the sounds of their increasingly aroused breathing, of hands against flesh, shaping, touching, caressing, of mouth against mouth, of tongues twining and seeking, were an erotic counterpoint to the uneven thud of their heartbeats.

Layer upon layer the passion built between them, with each breath, each unsteady pulsebeat taking her higher, Keira recognised. And Jay's touch fed its heat as his hands shaped her body and his mouth commanded her response.

Outside the storm still raged ignored—until a fiercely bright bolt of lightning flashed outside, briefly filling the room with a brilliant white light.

Keira tensed, dragging her mouth away from

Jay's to look uncertainly towards the window. Jay's gaze fastened on the rise and fall of Keira's breasts. The rapid movement of her chest dragged the wet fabric of her blouse against her skin, so that he could see her flesh beneath it. Keira wasn't looking at the window now. She was looking at him, her nipples dark and hard and straining as tightly against the wet silk of her bra as his erection was straining against his trousers.

The brilliance of the lightning faded, but the accuracy with which Jay found the place where the aureole of her nipple met the curve of her breast caused Keira to gasp out loud, her nipple hardening under the erotic touch of his thumb and forefinger.

'Look at me,' Jay commanded. He wanted to see her desire for him as well as feel it. He wanted to watch whilst the touch of his hands brought her pleasure. He wanted to see in her eyes what could not be hidden or denied by any verbal rejection.

In the shadowy semi-light Keira gave herself over to the flood of pleasure storming through her, her eyes liquid gold with arousal and her lips stung soft and swollen from his kisses as she looked up at Jay.

Just the heat engendered by the way Jay was looking back at her should surely have been enough to melt the clothes from her flesh, leaving her naked and open to his touch in all the ways she wanted it to be, Keira thought helplessly.

The lightning might have faded, softening the room back into darkness, but its brief life had lasted long enough for Jay to be able to reach unerringly for the buttons on Keira's blouse.

He heard her whimper, then felt her shudder when he tugged the wet fabric away from her skin, allowing her to sway closer to him, her naked breasts openly ready for the possession of his hands.

Could this really be her? Moaning, wantonly arching her back, pushing her body hungrily and rhythmically against Jay's touch? Keira wondered dizzily. Fierce spasms of pleasure surged through her, urging her to demand more. The caress of his hands on her breasts was making her ache unbearably for the touch of his lips against them, for the stroke of his tongue, the possessive, sensual suckling of her flesh that she knew would ignite a need in her that would change her for ever. Just thinking about it was making the pulse deep inside her grow, wanting the stroke of his fingers.

'Does this pleasure you? Do you want more?'

She was beyond speech—beyond anything other than giving herself over to him completely.

Keira didn't know whether or not she had spoken, but she did know that a message had been given and understood. And now they were both tugging at one another's clothes, interspersing their actions with kisses and caresses and, in her case, soft, fevered, delighted little moans of pleasure as she discovered some new bit of him to touch.

Who could have known that rain-wet flesh could feel so erotic, or that such an intensity of urgency could possess her?

Jay's hands were shaping her naked body, stroking down to her thighs and then up over her. His fingertips, spanning the smoothness of her bottom and then lifting her so that he could press her into his arousal, had her raking her nails down the length of his upper arm, whilst she sobbed her sexual heat into the wet flesh of his throat.

Had she parted her own thighs in open willingness, soliciting his long and deliberately erotic exploration of her intimate flesh, or had Jay parted them himself?

Keira had no idea, and she cared even less. She couldn't think or exist beyond the sensual stroke of his fingertip backwards and forwards over her clitoris.

Possessed by the desire that had materialised as quickly as the storm, Keira tugged and tore at Jay's clothes, shuddering with blatant sexual pleasure at each touch of his hands on her naked rain-sleek skin, moaning her delight and inciting more intimacy as each touch fuelled her hunger for more.

Here in this room, filled with the heat they themselves had generated, it felt almost as though the storm had ripped from her all her inhibitions.

Jay wasn't touching her any more; he wasn't

giving her that almost too intense pleasure, and its loss was making her tremble and ache. But before Keira could voice her loss Jay was picking her up and carrying her to the wide bed.

Keira clung to him as he lowered her onto the mattress, pressing passionate kisses on his throat and then his chest, her golden eyes brilliant with what it meant to be the woman he had aroused within her.

The storm had laid bare her feelings, both physical and emotional. She couldn't hide from them any more She had fallen in love with Jay.

He pushed her back on the bed and then kissed her mouth, slowly and deeply, until her senses swam and her nipples stiffened achingly into the palms of his hands. She welcomed the heat of his mouth as he kissed his way along the curve of her breast to circle first one nipple and then the other with the tip of his tongue.

The pulse deep inside her turned into a thudding, knowing, gnawing ache that leapt to the touch of Jay's fingers and responded rhythmically to their caress.

He moved back down the bed, circling her

slim ankle with his hand and lifting her leg so that he could string kisses from the inside of her ankle bone all the way along her leg to her knee, and then beyond, up over her thigh, whilst she trembled violently with a pleasure her body could not contain.

The thunder and lightning was inside her, possessing her, tossing her from one peak of pleasure to the next. Somehow her feet were on his shoulders. Somehow her body lay open to him to explore and enjoy as he wished. Keira gasped as his fingertips stroked through the parted wetness of the inner lips of her sex and her clitoris over and over again, slowly, then faster, moving over her and within her, taking her up so high, so fast, that she could barely draw breath between her shocked gasp of recognition and the sob of pleasure that convulsed her throat muscles at exactly the same time as Jay's caresses convulsed her body into the sharp intense spasm of her orgasm.

The pleasure, so swift and savage, clung to her in an aftermath of intense sweetness and emotional sensitivity that left her trembling, and Jay looked down at her. Her body felt weightless and boneless, and yet at the same time so heavy with exhaustion that she couldn't move. Overcome by her emotions, Keira reached for Jay's hand and pressed it fervently to her lips in an age-old gesture of intense love.

She was good—even better than he had expected. Taking her pleasure with a direct simplicity that had acted on him like a powerful aphrodisiac. He wanted to see that pleasure again. He wanted to watch whilst he gave it to her and she took it. He wanted her legs wrapped around him whilst he took her, stroking slowly and deeply into her, until she begged him to move faster and deeper, until she took him with her to that place she had just been… But, unexpectedly, she was practically falling asleep as he held her.

Frowning, Jay lowered her onto the bed and watched as her eyes closed.

It was the sound of running water that woke Keira—that, and a sense of loss because even in sleep she had known that Jay had left her.

The room was still dark, although the storm had gone. A shaft of oblong light from the half-open bathroom door coupled with the sound of the shower told her where Jay had gone.

She got up out of bed and padded naked towards the bathroom. Black marble covered the floor, its richness reflected in the ornately panelled mirrored walls. One half of the bathroom was almost filled with a large rectangular bath, sunk into the floor and reached via a set of marble steps. The other side of the room had been turned into the equivalent of a modern wet room, separated from the bathing area by a vanity unit and a glass screen. Jay was standing beneath the shower in the wet-room area, with his back to her.

Soapsuds and water glistened on his skin. Keira's heart and body contracted on a surge of love for him. She watched him for as long as she could bear to be apart from him, and then ran to him.

Jay turned as she reached the shower, looking at her and then taking her in his arms, kissing her slowly and sweetly, and then less slowly as she pressed herself closer to him.

Keira scooped some of the lather off his body and rubbed it against her own, watching the way the colour of his eyes burned from grey to silver as he poured shower gel into his palm and then slowly applied it to her body.

Ten minutes later, when the foam had disappeared along with the shower water, Keira knew that the desire Jay's touch had aroused in her was nowhere close to disappearing. Quite the opposite.

Slowly and wonderingly she reached out to touch him, running her fingertips along his breastbone and then down his body, through the soft dark hair that thickened around the base of his hardness.

Her chest rose and then fell sharply as her senses responded to the intimacy of her exploration, and uncertainly she stroked delicately along the rigid shaft.

Jay shuddered. What Keira was doing to him was sheer torment, and she must know it. He wanted to be enclosed by her, to be held firm, to feel her body embracing and caressing him. He wanted to take her and hold her and thrust deep into her. He wanted to feel her body's desire for his. He wanted to lose himself in her. He wanted…

Keira could feel the heavy, uneven thud of Jay's heartbeat, could taste the unique hot salt of his skin. 'I want you,' she told him, breathing the words out against his skin, the raw uneven huskiness of her voice matching the unsteadiness of her heartbeat. 'Make love to me, Jay.'

Her hands flat against the hard muscles of his six-pack, she placed a line of kisses down his body, her lips moving lower until finally she placed a kiss of love and longing against the smooth, rigid hardness of the flesh that pulsed beneath the hold of her hand.

At last she had done it—had begged him as he had sworn that she would. His pride was appeased. And only just in time, Jay acknowledged. He wasn't prepared to admit even to himself just how very few seconds more he would have lasted before his desire for her overwhelmed him and he had been the one begging her.

Now Jay couldn't wait any longer. He swept her up into his arms and carried her back to the bed.

His desire to finish what they had begun drove through the barriers he normally imposed on himself, so that his lovemaking wasn't confined to the mere physical skill he normally used to ensure his partner's pleasure whilst he himself remained emotionally detached. That detachment was replaced with something he could neither control nor reject, that swept and burned through him, taking possession of him.

Keira herself was lost—totally and completely. All that mattered was Jay and what she was feeling. There was no room for anything else. Together they filled her senses and her thoughts. His lovemaking had taken her to the heights already tonight. Now he was showing her that there were heights beyond those heights—unimaginable peak after peak of such exquisite sensual pleasures that they burned her senses like a brand. Jay's brand, she thought dizzily.

Keira was oblivious to the rustle of foil as Jay fought to control himself long enough to practise safe sex, knowing only that he had moved away from her. Wantonly she urged him back to her, with soft pleas interspersed with hungry kisses and caresses.

The return of the hard weight of him between her thighs made her shudder and arch up against him, her hands gripping his shoulders as he moved against her, thrusting slowly into her.

How could there be such an intensity of pleasure? It was driving her forward to meet it, to meet him, as he filled her body, possessing it—possessing her. It grew and sharpened, and an urgent, compelling need rushed through her, refusing to be checked, matching its pace to Jay's deepening thrusts.

The world—no, the universe, *his* universe, Jay acknowledged, had become the feel of Keira's flesh enclosing him, the feel of being with her and within her. This was all that mattered—the only thing that mattered. He thrust deeper, and felt the barrier that barred his way. The *barrier?* She was a *virgin?* How could she possibly be a virgin? Disbelief, followed by anger, followed by outrage, burned through him.

Why had Jay gone so still? That wasn't what she wanted. Keira moved eagerly against him, covering his mouth with her own, showing him with the hot, urgent thrust of her tongue just what she did want.

Caught totally off guard by his discovery, and by the way it changed the dynamics of what was happening, Jay wanted to withdraw from Keira. But both her body and his own were conspiring to prevent him from doing so. Her flesh clung wantonly to his, enclosing and possessing him in its soft moist heat, overwhelming what his brain wanted his body to do. His body had very different ideas. He moved, intending to pull back, but Keira moved with him, and within the space of one sharp indrawn breath it was too late for him to stop—too late for him to do anything but submit to the demands of their shared desire.

This time the pleasure was different, Keira recognized: deeper, stronger, its convulsions tightening around Jay's flesh and holding him there until her orgasm became his, and his hers. Until she was stormed, swept, elevated to a place beyond any place she had ever thought could exist, to a depth of intensity that shocked her as much as it pleasured her.

CHAPTER TEN

A VIRGIN—how could she have been a virgin? Jay stared grimly into the darkness whilst Keira slept at his side. It angered and disturbed him that all his preconceptions about her had been so very wrong, and that as a virgin she had been so far from his original assessment of her. It angered him that his judgement of her had been so glaringly wrong. He felt betrayed by his own inability to assess her correctly, and further angered by the belief that she would now have expectations and ambitions that he had no intention of fulfilling. Had he known the truth about her he would have warned her off, making sure that they did not have sex. By concealing her true sexual experience from him, or rather her lack of it, she had allowed him to go on believing what he had, putting him in an untenable situation. Deliberately?

Twenty-something virgins had by definition to have a pretty heavy agenda going on. Either they had sexual hang-ups or problems—which patently she most certainly did not—or there was another reason. And the only logical reason Jay could think of was that Keira had remained a virgin because she expected to exchange her virginity for commitment. That was never going to happen. He had no intention of making a commitment to any woman—ever. During the years of their estrangement his father had let him know many times via his courtiers that he wanted to make plans to arrange a suitable marriage for him, but in that both he and Rao had withstood their parent, refusing to submit to a marriage of tradition and royal necessity.

Rao would, of course, ultimately have to marry, and his wife would have to be someone worthy of being his Maharani. For himself, Jay knew that it would be expected if he did marry that he too would marry a suitable bride. But he had no intention of marrying—not anyone, not ever. So Keira had wasted her virginity on him and he would have to tell her so. There must not be any more errors of judgement or aspiration.

Slowly, like wisps of fine cloud, memories of the night drifted back to him. Keira whispering his name to him, thanking him for her pleasure, her eyes huge with emotion.

Emotion. Jay's mouth compressed. What had happened between them had nothing to do with emotion—at least not on his part—and the sooner he told her that the better. Both for her sake as well as his own. The last thing he wanted was to have her start building some ridiculous fantasy out of what had quite simply been a single night of sex—and one that he had no intention of repeating. He would have to speak to her before the situation got even more out of hand than it was already.

Keira had been awake for some time, lying in bed and marvelling at the difference between the woman she had been and the woman she was now. Her body glowed still with the aftermath of her pleasure. *Their* pleasure, she reminded herself. Jay would know now that he had been wrong about her, and that what she felt for him was unique, something she had never shared with anyone else. She was still on a physical and emotional high from last night, in a blessed-out state where the world felt like a fairytale come true and she its heroine princess. And all because of Jay.

Jay! Where was he? What would he say to her? What would she say to him? Her heart was thumping unsteadily. Already she missed him. Already she ached for him and wanted to be with him. Already the effect of the night's sexual intimacy had changed her and their relationship, and her heart was speeding on wings into a magical world where everything and anything was possible.

It was Jay himself who brought her back down to earth, arriving with a tray of tea and an expression that had her giddy heart's headlong race brought to an abrupt halt.

Something was wrong. Something was more than wrong. Jay was looking autocratic and distant. He was fully dressed. He didn't come to her, or even sit down on the bed beside her, instead he walked over to the window and then turned to face her so that its light fell on her face but obscured his.

'I owe you an apology. And I'm afraid it will have to be accompanied by a warning.'

He was speaking to her as though he was addressing a business meeting, Keira recognised, his whole manner cool and distant. Her heart was pounding again—but not this time with elation. Instead what she felt was dread.

'I want to be frank with you, Keira. Had I known you were a virgin I would never have had sex with you. Were you a girl of eighteen or so, I would add here that I understand you might have had rosy romantic delusions about men falling passionately in love with sweet innocent virgins, and throwing their heart and an offer of marriage at their feet having taken that virginity. But you are not eighteen. You are twenty-seven. Women of twenty-seven do not remain virgins by accident or out of some romantic delusion. To have chosen virginity when yours is such a sensual and passionate nature can't have been easy.'

Keira's mouth had gone dry. She might not have been expecting quite the eighteen-year-old's scenario he had described with such sparing and cruel accuracy, but to be addressed as Jay was addressing her now was a horrible shock and very hurtful.

'My assumption has to be that you chose virginity because you saw it as, shall we say, a good business decision—an insurance policy that would mature with handsome dividends when it was offered to your chosen recipient: your exclusivity sexually, both past and future, in exchange for the right kind of marriage. I do not doubt that there are men, wealthy men, who are willing to make such a barter in return for the security that comes from knowing that their wife is indeed a model of virtue. However, I am not one of those men. To be blunt, I have no intention of making a commitment to any woman ever, either inside marriage or outside it, and had you told me the truth about yourself first, I would have suggested that you retained your virginity to bestow on someone else. Sexually, what we shared last night was very enjoyable, but that was all it was for me. A fleeting enjoyment which is now over and will be quickly forgotten. I am sorry if my words offend or upset you, but it is better that you know the truth. It would be cruel of me indeed to allow you to hope for something I have no intention of giving you or anyone else.'

Keira felt each word like a blow to her heart and her pride. He was both wrong about her and right. She had not set out to use her virginity to force him into a commitment, but she *had* given it up to him because she herself had made an emotional commitment to him. He must never know that, though. Not now. For her pride's sake she had to salvage what she could of the situation and her self-respect.

It did not help that she was lying naked under the bedclothes whilst he was fully dressed. Didn't it tell her all she really needed to know about him that even now, when he was humiliating her, he had taken for himself every advantage there was to be had in order to give himself more power than her. He was dressed; she wasn't. He had the light behind him; she had it on her. He had had time to plan and rehearse what he intended to say; she had not. Well, luckily for her, living with her great-aunt had taught her a great deal about how to defend herself when she was the weaker party.

She pulled the bedclothes securely around her body and sat up.

'I appreciate what you're saying,' she told him, trying to keep her voice as cool and focused as his had been, 'but I must tell you that once again you've reached a conclusion about me that isn't correct.'

There was a telling silence during which Keira waited, praying that he wouldn't tell her outright that he didn't believe her.

His assessing, 'Meaning?' had her exhaling unsteadily.

'Meaning that, yes, I had chosen to remain a virgin, but the reason I did so had nothing whatsoever with any desire on my part to get married. Far from it.'

He had moved slightly, but she still could not see his face.

'You remained a virgin because you don't

want to get married? Forgive me, but I have to say that I don't…'

Any minute now he was going to start asking questions she could not answer. She had to head him off with something plausible.

'I wanted a career and my own independence, and as a teenager it seemed to me that as soon as a girl fell in love she stopped wanting those things. So I vowed not to fall in love. It was far too dangerous. Remaining a virgin was a by-product of my decision not to fall in love.'

She gave what she hoped was a convincingly careless small shrug.

'Obviously as I've grown older I've been able to recognise that it is possible to have sex and remain emotionally independent, and I had begun to wonder what I might be missing because of a decision made when I was very immature.'

'And you've been looking round for someone to experience sex with? Is that what you're trying to say?'

Keira actually managed to laugh.

'I hadn't got as far as that, and if I had done

there would have been the embarrassment of my virginity to deal with. I'm old enough to understand that what happened between us was something that neither of us expected to happen and that both of us would probably have preferred not to have happened.'

There had been the clear ring of truth in her voice when she had spoken about her vow not to fall in love and her fear of doing so, Jay acknowledged. He had already misjudged her once. His pride didn't want him doing so a second time. It made sense for him to accept what she was saying, but at the same time he still intended to reinforce his own message to her by putting things on a strictly business footing.

'It might be best in the circumstances if we terminated our contract,' Keira told him. She couldn't afford to break it herself, but she was hoping desperately now that *he* would terminate it. How on earth was she going to be able to work for him now feeling as she did about him? *Feeling* as she did about him? What did that mean?

'I do not wish to terminate our contract,' Jay was telling her sharply. 'It would be too costly and disruptive to find another interior designer at this stage. That is in part why I am speaking with you as I am. I don't want there to be any misunderstandings—any hopes or aspirations, shall we say, that cannot be met.'

Keira permitted herself a small, bitter inward smile as she imagined what he would think if he knew the truth about her.

'All my hopes and aspirations are focused on my business.'

'As mine are on mine,' Jay responded.

Jay had gone. She was on her own, but even now Keira did not dare to give way to her emotions—just as she had never dared to do so when she had lived with her great-aunt.

To allow anyone to see her pain was to risk having it used against her, to hurt her even more. She had learned that lesson very young. But the pain she had experienced then was nothing compared to what she must somehow find a way to live through now.

The unthinkable, the unbearable, the most cruel of all cruelties had infiltrated her defences and overpowered her. She had fallen in love with Jay. But he must never know that. She would die before she would humiliate herself by letting him see what a fool she had been.

Last night she had broken the most important promise she had ever made to herself. Now she must face the consequences, she told herself bleakly.

CHAPTER ELEVEN

HER work on the first three of the show houses was finished, and there was no real need for her to be here at this hour of the morning, straightening cushions, checking on the arrangement of flowers and the drape of curtains, but Keira was desperate to keep herself busy. Jay was due back from Mumbai today.

Was she going to be strong enough not to betray any reaction to his return? He had, after all, made the situation plain enough to her. From the moment he had questioned her about her virginity to the moment he had left for Mumbai he had treated her with clinical detachment. She, meanwhile, had gone through hurt to anger and back to hurt again, and it had been a relief of sorts when he had actually left.

At least with him gone she had been able to

get on with her work without the fear of what his proximity might do to her self control.

But soon he would be back. And last night her dreams had been filled with her longing for him—so much so, in fact, that her body now ached physically and tormentingly for him.

He had emailed her to tell her that he was bringing with him the art director of a new swish homes magazine, with a view to the magazine doing a feature on the development— complete with photographs of her interiors and an interview with her on modern interior design and décor.

Keira had dressed appropriately for the interview in one of her favourite silk linen outfits, a softly styled cream skirt teamed with a toning strappy top under a wrap cardigan. She had completed her outfit with a pair of designer sunglasses and a fashionably large leather bag—a gift from an up and coming young designer whose apartment she had once styled for a photoshoot.

She had read recently in *Vogue* that the handbag was now a top 'must have' fashion item.

Would Jay be pleased with the work she had done? She tried to see the rooms through his eyes instead of her own. Her hands were trembling slightly as she straightened the piece of polished wood artwork she had placed on the glass-topped coffee table. What was she going to do if he didn't like it? Burst into tears? Hardly.

What she wanted him to see was his in-control interior designer, not a needy, over-emotional woman who had fallen in love with him.

She couldn't stay here all day. She needed to return to the palace. Jay hadn't been specific in his e-mail as to the timing of his return.

She was just on the point of leaving the show house when a four-wheel-drive drew up outside, and Jay and another man climbed out of it.

Keira felt as though her heart had physically stopped beating, as though the earth itself had stopped moving—because, like her, it was so focused on this one man that nothing else could exist.

The ache that had taken possession of her heart now spread to the rest of her body, so that every part of her that had touched him or been touched by him longed violently for that physical contact once more.

He was coming towards her, turning his head so that he could look at her. To make sure that she still understood what he had told her? Keira forced her lips into a professional smile, no different for Jay than it was for the man to whom he was introducing her, who was now smiling at her with male warmth and interest that threw into sharp relief Jay's coldness towards her.

'My friends call me Bas,' he told her, 'and I hope that you will do the same. I have heard a great many complimentary things about your work, and I am looking forward to featuring it in our magazine.'

'I expect Jay has already told you that part of his remit was that he wanted me to use local products as much as possible?' Keira asked him as she stepped to one side to allow the two men to enter the show house.

'Do you feel that interfered with your own creativity?'

'No, not at all. Using local products and

focusing on the nature of the land around the development was very much in keeping with my own way of working. I enjoyed finding different ways to stick to Jay's remit, but at the same time ensure that the houses reflect the lifestyles and tastes of the people who will buy the properties.'

Keira stopped speaking to allow the art director to look at the décor and inspect what she had done.

'I'm impressed,' he told her. 'Very impressed. This toile, for instance…'

'Locally made and designed.'

'Jay, with your permission I'd like to make Keira and the work she's done here a lead feature in our magazine. In fact I'd love to devote an entire magazine to what's going on here, with interviews with the local craftsmen, articles on the history of those crafts, that kind of thing. What's happening here really is revolutionary. Now that I've seen what Keira's done I'm really blown away.'

Jay was frowning, and Keira wondered if perhaps he wasn't as pleased with the interiors as she had hoped.

'What I need to do is get a crew up here and some interviews set up. I know you want the feature to coincide with the launch of the development via your own advertising. You said you'd be launching officially at the World Trade Fair in six months' time? Keira, I'll want to do an in-depth interview with you, and I'd like to get an idea of how you work. Would it be okay with you if I attached myself to you and followed you around for the next couple of days?'

Jay was frowning even more now.

'Well, if Jay doesn't mind...' she told Bas helplessly.

'Of course he doesn't mind. That's what he's brought me down here for—isn't it, Jay?'

Ignoring the other man, Jay turned to Keira and said tersely, 'Come and see me in my office at the palace in an hour's time. I want to go through a few things with you. I'll take you to your hotel now, Bas, and leave you there to get yourself settled in.'

The art director smiled warmly at Keira.

'It's only a flying visit for me this time, but

I'm already looking forward to coming back and getting to spend more time with you.'

At least someone had admired the work she had done, even if that someone wasn't Jay, Keira thought sadly as she waited for the houseboy to come back from telling Jay that she was here to see him.

She had arrived early for their appointment, and now she was feeling slightly sick and very nervous. The only thing that was keeping her going was her pride—and her determination to prove to Jay that she could be utterly professional.

Rakesh had returned and was asking her to follow him.

With every step that took her closer to Jay's office and Jay himself her apprehension increased, until she would have given anything to turn and run away. What if he told her that he knew how she felt about him? What would she do then? How would she survive that humiliation?

Rakesh had knocked on the door and was pushing it open for her. It was too late now for her to run away. Keira stepped into the room, and then froze as she realised that Jay was standing so near to the door that she had virtually walked straight into him. When he reached past her to shut the door she felt close to dizziness with the effort of not allowing her body to react to his proximity. It was like depriving her lungs of oxygen, leaving her feeling dangerously weak and off balance. She had missed him so much. She ached for him so much. But she must not feel like this—she must not *be* like this.

'Has Bas asked you to go to bed with him yet?'

The words, delivered in a harsh, flat and yet distinctly antagonistic voice, shocked her out of her painful thoughts.

'No, of course not.'

'There is no *of course not* about it,' Jay told her. 'He wants you. He made that perfectly obvious.'

This kind of discussion was the last thing she had expected, and she had no idea how to deal with it.

'If you're concerned that I might prejudice the success of your development by behaving unprofessionally—' she began, but Jay cut ruthlessly across what she was saying.

'You don't want him, then?' he demanded.

'No, I don't.'

'Do you want me?'

It was several betraying seconds before she could find the breath to speak.

'No.'

'Do you want me to *make* you want me?'

Now she was panicking. 'I'm not staying here to listen to any more of this.'

He reached the door before her, blocking her escape, leaving her with nowhere to go other than into his arms.

His kiss was fiercely possessive and even more fiercely sexual, with the tip of his tongue as it probed the soft line of her lips mirroring the hard urgency of his erection. His hands were caressing her breasts, shaping her body to his own. A few more heartbeats and she would be totally lost, not caring one bit about the promises she had made to herself.

'I want you in my bed.'

Keira made herself resist the lure of his words.

'Because you think another man wants me?' she challenged him.

'No—although I admit seeing him looking at you the way he was made me decide that I'd better not waste any time putting my proposition to you.'

The word 'proposition' struck a chill note against Keira's heart and her overheated senses.

Jay had released her now, and was telling her bluntly, 'Sex in my office has never had much appeal for me, but if I don't put some distance between us I can't promise you that it isn't going to happen. The next time you and I have sex I want to have the time and the privacy to ensure that it's a very special and memorable experience—and for all the right reasons.'

Her heart was thumping unsteadily now, her body reacting to the promise contained in his words in a way that made total nonsense of her vow to herself to remain in control.

'You as good as said that you aren't into virgins,' she reminded him.

'You aren't a virgin any more. Look, the

reality is that whether we like it or not there's a sexual attraction between us that I'm prepared to admit is far stronger than I'd allowed for. It's certainly strong enough to have kept me awake at night wanting you whilst I've been away— wanting only you. We both know the score: no long-term relationship, no commitment, no emotional trauma. But that doesn't mean that we can't be bed partners. My guess is that you want me every bit as much as I want you, and my proposition to you is that we give ourselves a break and ride the wave together rather than fight against it. The kind of intense sexual hunger we're experiencing burns itself out quickly once its satisfied. Right now by resisting it all we're doing is feeding it. Far better to enjoy it, and one another, for the short duration of its lifetime—don't you agree?'

Oh, yes, she agreed. She'd always loved living dangerously— *not*! Keira couldn't think of anything more calculated to destroy her than becoming Jay's 'bed partner'. She knew that as soon as he stopped wanting her physically he would want her out of his life. She knew that he felt nothing whatsoever emotionally for her, that all he wanted from her was sex. And yet, shamefully, she was desperately tempted to agree—just to have the pleasure he was offering her and the memories it would give her.

If she refused, how was she going to feel ten years from now? Twenty years from now and more? Knowing that she could have had this time with him but had refused it out of fear of the emotional pain she knew must come with it. And wasn't there another concern she ought to consider? a sly inner voice pointed out to her. If she refused mightn't Jay start to suspect that she was refusing because she had fallen in love with him?

'Have dinner with me tonight,' Jay suggested. 'You can give me your answer then.'

'Very well.'

Keira marvelled that she could sound so calm and matter of fact.

'We'll have dinner in my private quarters, here at the palace.'

Now she was panicking—and excited, and aroused...

* * *

What did one wear to have dinner with a man when that dinner was a prelude to that man taking you to bed? It wasn't a situation Keira had ever been in before. She had never had cause to dress for seduction. Images of low-cut balcony bras trimmed with lace and itsy-bitsy pieces of silk and lace masquerading as knickers floated through her head. Her underwear was of the smooth, no-VPL nude colour variety, far more functional than it was sexy.

She remembered that she had seen a shop in the bazaar, selling ethereally delicate and diaphanous harem pants and beaded bra tops. Would Jay appreciate her dressing up like a Bollywood dancing girl? Somehow she thought he was too sophisticated for that kind of obvious 'bedroom' outfit. So what did a woman who was going to be a man's non-permanent sexual partner wear pre-foreplay? Was there a set 'uniform'? Tailored clothes and no underwear *à la* Sharon Stone, perhaps? Keira didn't think she was quite ready to be quite so 'up front', as it were.

In the end, having decided that for her own

sense of self-respect she should be herself—or at least as much herself as she could be given that Jay must not know how she felt about him—Keira opted for a simple loose-fitting cream dress and a pair of cream sandals. Her skin gleamed silkily with the light tan it had developed, and since this was definitely not a business meeting Keira left her hair down, to swing softly on her shoulders. She wasn't a fan of excessive make-up, using only a light touch of mascara and lipstick, and she was glad that she had opted for a simple casual appearance when unexpectedly Jay himself came to escort her to dinner. She discovered, on opening the door to him, that he too was dressed casually, wearing an unstructured linen shirt open at the throat and a pair of jeans.

It was hard not to show what she was feeling, and even harder to look as relaxed as Jay himself obviously was as he smiled at her and told her, 'I thought we'd walk back through the gardens.' He looked down at her feet as he spoke, presumably to check that she was wearing suitable garden-walking footwear, and yet Keira felt the most intense surge of sensual heat flood through her as he focused on her bare toes with their pale pink–polished nails.

He couldn't possibly know that she had been reading the *Kama Sutra* since he had mentioned it to her—any more than he could know how much her sexual senses had been awakened by what she had read and the realisation of the many opportunities the human body provided for shared sexual pleasure. It had been a painful learning curve in many ways, reinforcing for her both how much she loved and wanted Jay and how much it hurt knowing that she would never share those pleasures with him.

Only now she would. Her spirits soared and flew. When Jay reached for her hand she put her own into his and smiled at him. Immediately his hand tightened on hers.

'Do you realise how much you are tempting me when you smile like that?'

'Like what?'

'Like you can't wait to be in my arms.'

'I…' Keira paused There were a hundred and more smart, sassy responses she could give him, but only one of them really mattered. There were so many reasons why she should not be honest with him. But she couldn't help herself. 'I can't,' she told him simply.

He had been stroking her fingers, but now he stopped. Keira could feel the heat they were both generating pressing in on them, wrapping them in an invisible cloak of sensual longing.

'Rakesh will have brought our dinner.'

'Then we'd better go and eat it.'

Simple words, and yet the messages their other senses were exchanging went far deeper and were far more intimate.

Dusk was stealing the light and the heat from the gardens, cloaking them in soft shadows. Keira didn't know whether to be relieved or disappointed when Jay didn't pause to kiss her as he guided her to the steps that led up to his private quarters and took her into a traditionally styled salon with low-lying divans drawn up around a table. Jewel-coloured glass lamps illuminated the room in rich reds and ambers, and scented smoke perfumed the air. The strains of soft music echoed softly through the scented darkness, brushing against Keira's senses like a physical touch. This was foreplay *Kama Sutra*-style, and already she was captivated and entranced.

When Jay led her to one of the divans and took the one adjacent to it himself she lay as he had done, so that their heads were almost touching. But she still wasn't prepared for it when he reached for one of the bowls on the table and dipped into it, feeding her a small ball of rice flavoured with saffron and stuffed with plump sultanas. It was all so shockingly erotic: the intimacy of being fed by him, the touch of his fingers against her lips, the scent of his body as he leaned closer to her. All of it—and most of all when he suggested softly to her, 'Why don't you feed me?'

Her fingers were trembling when she lifted the rice to his lips, and her whole body was trembling by the time he had taken it from her, his fingers closing round her wrist to hold her as he licked her fingers, slowly and deliberately.

After that Keira had an appetite for only one

thing. Although she did manage to eat the small juicy strawberries Jay fed her before finally losing her self-control and pressing her lips to his fingers and then his palm.

As though it was a signal he had been waiting for, Jay stood up and held out his hand to her. Silently Keira took it. Her heart was thumping heavily. In the jewelled shadows of the scented room Jay pulled her closer, and then traced the shape of her face with his fingertips. When he reached her mouth Keira's lips parted automatically, her tongue-tip caressing his flesh before she sucked his fingers into her mouth.

Jay's free hand was on her breast, his fingers stroking her nipple, and when she sucked on his fingers he reciprocated by plucking erotically at her nipple. Keira sucked harder and was rewarded in kind. She stroked her tongue over his fingertips and then shuddered in wild delight when Jay bent his head and placed his mouth over her fabric-covered breast, his tongue probing the hard jut of her nipple. How could something so simple arouse her to such intense pleasure?

She could feel her heat beating impatiently

inside her body. She could feel her body pulsing, softening, opening in eager liquid longing. It was too late now to regret her prim decision not to take the shameless step of abandoning her underwear, too late to wish that she had done exactly that so all Jay had to do to satisfy the hungry ache inside her was slide his hand inside her dress and then—Keira shuddered wildly when, just as though she had spoken her wanton longing out loud, Jay put his hand on her thigh. Not, as she quickly discovered, to touch her intimately, but instead so that he could pick her up and carry her into the bedroom, where he placed her down on his bed.

Now his fingertip tracing of her flesh began again—but not this time on her face. Instead it was her body he was touching, tracing, with those light, delicate touches that somehow inflamed her senses far more than anything more heavy-handed could have done.

Long before he was kneeling beside her, cupping her now bare foot in his hand, Keira had lost the fight to retain her self-control and had given herself over completely to his keeping.

Her body was an instrument, tuned only to respond to his touch, and from it he was now drawing a pleasure so intense that it verged on pain. If he were to stop touching her now she would fall into an abyss of unsatisfied longing that would burn through her for ever, she decided wildly when his tongue tip traced the inner arch of her bare foot, sending fierce strobes of pleasure right up to the heart of her sex.

She had no memory of them removing their clothes, but they must have done since they were both now naked. Jay's body was lean and superbly muscled, its scent and taste given over into her possession as she touched and kissed him as intimately as she dared, stroking her fingertips over his rigidly erect sex and marvelling at its sensitivity to her touch and its capacity for response.

Jay was caressing the inside of her thighs, encouraging them to fall open and offer him the hidden mystery of her body. Like the petals of a lily, opening to the heat of the sun, the lips of her sex curved and swelled open at his touch, slick against her body's eager, ready wetness.

The pulse deep inside her that had begun what felt like an eternity ago quickened and deepened into an urgent ache. Jay's deliberate caress against her clitoris provoked a low moan from her throat, and an agonized, *'Don't...'* causing Jay to frown.

'You want me to stop?' he asked her.

'Only because I want you inside me, and I'm afraid that if you don't stop it's going to be too late.'

That was as close as she could get to telling him that she suspected she was about to orgasm, but it was obvious that he knew what she was trying to say. He covered the whole of her sex with his hand and then repositioned himself, bending his head to kiss her and then sliding his hands beneath her to lift her, so that her legs were on his shoulders. He moved slowly and deliberately into her, with carefully paced thrusts that took him deeper and deeper and had Keira crying out with fierce pleasure as she rose to meet him, picking up his rhythm until she was the one taking him deeper, holding him there so that her body could take its pleasure of him, tightening around him to caress and enjoy him before eagerly urging him further.

'Faster,' she told him. 'Deeper—deeper, Jay.' Her voice trembled, like her, on the edge of the precipice as Jay gathered himself and waited until Keira's cries told him that she could wait no longer.

As the world swung on its axis and a million darts of pleasure exploded inside her like so many fireworks, Keira clung desperately to Jay.

Her face wet with tears of completion, she told him brokenly, 'That was wonderful.'

'That is just the start,' Jay told her as he wiped away her tears with his thumb-pad. 'There will be many, many wonderful times for us, and many wonders for us to explore together and share.'

CHAPTER TWELVE

JAY had been right. As the days had turned into weeks and the weeks into months—three of them, to be exact—there had been many wonderful times. There had been night after night during which she had thought she had climbed the heights, only to discover those heights had been mere foothills of pleasure.

Jay was an expertly sensual teacher, and Keira admitted she was a very eager pupil—his pleasure her own and hers his.

There had been nights when they had lain on the divans and Jay had shown her the beautifully illustrated plates in the ancient copy of the *Kama Sutra* he had told her he had bought as a young man in a bazaar. It had originally been the property of a maharaja whose library had been sold, he had explained to her, and was of immense cultural and financial value.

He had read the text to her, his voice sensually soft and erotic as he stroked the words as delicately as he stroked her skin. Uncertainly at first, but then with growing confidence, Keira had studied the illustrated plates whilst Jay encouraged her to choose a position she found erotically exciting so that they could experience it together. Jay had teased her that they should go through the alphabet, that every night they should pick a different letter and a different position. But some nights they would have run through half a dozen letters before dawn had streaked the sky, and others they would have enjoyed only one, taking their pleasure over and over again.

Against all her expectations—and Keira suspected Jay's as well—his desire for her, far from burning itself out, had actually increased.

When he had to be away from her on business, his return often resulted in him breaking his rule of not having sex in his office, such was the intensity of his physical desire for her.

His *physical* desire for her, Keira reminded herself sadly. Because that was all he felt for her. Physical desire.

There had been pleasure beyond any pleasure she could ever have imagined between them, but for her—hand in hand with that pleasure, measuring it step by step and now finally outweighing it—there had also been terrible pain. It was a pain that came not just from knowing that Jay would never return her feelings, but increasingly from her own unexpected and dangerous feelings of mingled guilt and pain about her past. Guilt because she had withheld the truth about it from Jay, and pain because she could never be her true self with him—because she couldn't ever know the kind of security that came from being accepted as she was.

The reality was that she was living not just one lie but several, and that could not go on. It was destroying her. She lived in fear of letting slip to Jay in the heat of their intimacy the fact that she loved him. She lived in fear of the ultimate ending of their relationship when he grew tired of her. And yet at the same time a part of her longed for the peace of mind that would come from knowing she would no longer need to lie by default.

She couldn't bear the thought of the rejection and contempt she would see in his eyes once he knew the truth about her. And she would see them. She knew that. She hadn't forgotten his attitude towards her when they had first met and he had mistakenly believed that she was the kind of woman willing to offer her body in return for material benefits.

Like mother, like daughter. How often had she heard those words from her great-aunt? They were branded into her—a curse that she carried with her, and a fear that would always haunt her.

She had given in to her own longing to be Jay's lover believing his desire for her would burn itself out in a matter of days—no more than a couple of weeks at most. She had judged that that was something she could survive for the sake of the pleasure it would give her and the memories she would have. But now it had been three months, and with each passing day her longing for what she could not have was growing stronger. Soon it would overwhelm her. Before that happened she had to leave.

Her work on the houses was finished. Jay had been away in Mumbai for the last three days, and in his absence she had forced herself to think about her own situation and to make the decision she knew she must make for her own sake.

Her bags were packed and her ticket for her flight home bought. In just over an hour's time she would be leaving for the airport in the taxi she had already booked. All she had to do was write the letter she had to leave for Jay, telling him that she had completed the work he had commissioned her to do, that she had enjoyed their time together, but that it was time for her to return to London and her own life and career.

He would soon find someone new to replace her in his bed.

Jay looked out of the window of his private yet as it touched down on the runway. He had no idea why he had felt this compulsion to conclude his business in Mumbai ahead of schedule. It wasn't, after all, the first time he had been apart from Keira during their relationship. His absences had served to increase their desire for one another, and his returns had brought new heights of pleasure for them both. Keira had never reacted to his absence with sulks or demands—nor had she ever indicated that she had missed him, or would have liked to have gone with him. There was no logical reason for him to feel this almost driven urgency to get back to her. She would be there, waiting to welcome him with the sensual eagerness of her body for his possession and her open delight in the pleasure he gave her.

She was the ideal bed partner: sensual and spirited, taking and giving pleasure in equal measure. It had surprised him how much, given the fact that she had been so inexperienced, and yet her acceptance of his terms for their relationship and its lack of any commitment had allowed him to let down his guard with her and show her his passion for her, safe in the knowledge that she came to him out of her own desire for him rather than any desire for what he could give her.

Maybe that was why he continued to want her so intensely long after he had expected to have had his fill of her.

He no longer read the *Kama Sutra* to her because now they had created their own personal repertoire of intimate pleasures— pleasures she had taken eagerly and adapted inventively to her own needs and to his, making them special and personal by the way she had put her own mark on them.

And on him?

Jay frowned. His thoughts were fast-tracking down a route that was becoming all too familiar. No commitment, he had said, and he had meant it. He still meant it.

His car was waiting for him. He preferred to drive himself. He removed his suit jacket, throwing it into the back of the car along with his laptop and his case.

He had seen Bas whilst he had been in Mumbai, and the art director was pressuring him to set up an interview with Keira. The advertising was booked for the launch of the development, and he had seen the photographs of the interiors and understood why the agency he had hired to market the development had been so enthusiastic about its success.

Keira had excelled his remit and produced something that was iconically stylish in concept and yet at the same time extremely liveable. Looking at the photographs, he had caught himself wondering what she might do with his London apartment, had even mentally visualised her living there in it with him. He pressed his foot down on the accelerator. In his pocket was a leather case from one of Mumbai's most exclusive jewellers, containing a pair of antique diamond wrist-cuffs. He had known the moment he had seen them that Keira would love them. They were unique. Just like her.

It was time for her to leave. She could put the letter on Jay's desk on her way out. Keira picked up her bag and reached for the handle of her trolley case.

Her bedroom door opened.

She swung round, the colour leaving her face as she saw Jay standing in the doorway, looking from her to the case and then back again.

His curt, 'What's going on?' didn't do anything to steady her nerves.

Keira knew that her voice was trembling as she told him unsteadily, 'My work here is finished…'

'Your work may be finished, but what about us?'

This was so much worse than she had expected. She must stay focused and be practical, not give in to her longing to beg him to make her stay.

'I have to earn my living, Jay.'

So he had been right all along. It had all been an elaborate set-up—a trick to bring him to this point. A sickening rush of bitter anger seized him. But it wasn't strong enough to stop him giving in and telling her harshly, 'Don't worry. I'll make it worth your while to stay. How much did you have in mind? Ten thousand a month?'

Keira couldn't speak or move. The ferocity of her pain gripped her. It was no good telling herself that she had known what he really thought of her, and that she had no one to blame but herself for the humiliation and anguish she was now suffering. She was, after all, her mother's daughter—wasn't she?

'Not enough? Well, how about if I throw this in as a sweetener?'

Jay reached into his jacket pocket and removed the jeweller's box, which he threw onto the chair close to where Keira was standing.

'Go ahead and open it,' he told her.

Keira felt as though her heart was shrivelling inside her chest, as if she was, in all the ways that really mattered, going through a form of emotional death. It was pointless reminding herself that she had known she would suffer. Knowing had not prepared her for the reality of that pain.

'I'm not for sale, Jay,' she told him. She felt leached of life and hope, her voice mirroring her feelings and recording her sense of emptiness and loss.

'No?'

'No.'

She thought that he was physically going to stop her from going. And to her shame a part of her actually hoped that he might, despite what he had just said and done. But, although he started to move towards her, he stopped short of reaching her.

She had to walk so close to him that she could almost feel and hear the angry thud of his heartbeat. That same heartbeat she had felt so many times against her own body, and wishing that it might match the love that filled her own heart for him.

Well, she knew now how impossible that was. All Jay wanted was to buy her for as long as he wanted her. That knowledge made her feel acutely sick.

The day she returned home Keira checked her accounts online and found that a very large sum of money indeed had been paid into her business account. Far more than was due to her from Jay on completion of the contract.

Keira e-mailed him, pointing out his error, and received an e-mail in return saying that the extra was 'for services rendered'. It would not be accepted if it was returned as he always paid his dues.

After she had finished crying Keira made out a cheque for the extra amount and gave it to a charity that helped rescue young women from prostitution, informing them that the money was a gift from Jay.

It was over. It should never have existed in the first place. But now it was over and she had to find a way to get on with her life.

CHAPTER THIRTEEN

SHE just hoped that her potential client kept their appointment, Keira thought as she walked through the entrance of the expensive and very exclusive boutique hotel suggested by the client as a meeting place. Far too exclusive and discreet to have anything as commercial as a foyer, its entrance hall was more like the entrance to a private home.

An elegantly dressed woman wearing what Keira suspected might be Chanel greeted her and suggested that she might like to wait in a private sitting room, overlooking their equally private garden.

The hotel had been designed by a very well-known design team and showed all their hallmark touches. Keira was impressed and envious.

It had been six weeks since she had left India,

and each one of them had felt like its own special version of hell.

Things had to get better. *She* had to get better. And she had to get over Jay. She had to stop loving him and wanting him. She had to.

'Hello, Keira.'

Jay! She stood up, and then had to sit down again as her legs refused to support her.

He looked thinner, with lines running from his nose to his mouth that were surely new—unless they were a trick of the light.

'I apologise for tricking you into coming here, but I couldn't think of any other way to get you to see me.' He put down the briefcase he was carrying. 'I've brought some press cuttings to show you, just in case you haven't already seen them. Your work on the houses has attracted rave reviews.'

'I'm glad the development has been a success.' How wooden and stilted her voice sounded—nothing like the voice in which she had told him of the pleasure he was giving her, the pleasure she had wanted him to go on giving her when they had been in bed together. The pain breaking inside her was unbearable, but it had to be borne. She could not escape from it.

'I owe you an apology.'

Could this really be Jay, actually sounding almost humble, actually attempting to be a penitent? Or was she simply imagining it?

'I've missed you, Keira.'

Now she *knew* she was imagining things.

Never in a hundred lifetimes would the Jay she knew have admitted to missing her.

He was looking at her patiently, waiting for her to say something.

'If you are trying to say that you want me back—' she began, only to have him shake his head.

'No, that isn't what I'm trying to say,' he told her crisply.

The hopes she had tried to pretend she didn't have crashed in on her. Why, why, *why* had she let herself hope so stupidly? Because she was a fool and she loved him, that was why.

'What I'm trying to say is that what I thought I wanted from life is not what I want at all. I've changed, Keira. You have changed me. From being a man who didn't want to commit to a woman at any price, I've become a man who would give every penny he possessed for the chance to make a commitment to one very special woman. And that woman is you. I've come to ask if you will give me a chance to show you how special what we've already shared is, and how much more special it can be. I want you—not just in my bed, Keira, but in my life, as my partner, my love, my one and only for all time. I want you to marry me.'

It was a dream. It had to be. This could not be Jay standing here saying these things to her. But it was.

'You can't mean it,' was all she could say.

'I *do* mean it. Perhaps the blow to my head that concussed me brought me to my senses— I don't know. I only know that when I came round in hospital all I wanted was to have you there with me.'

'Hospital? You've been hurt?'

Jay shrugged dismissively.

'A minor car collision—nothing serious. I was driving too fast, trying to escape the demons who were telling me I had just ruined my life, having driven away the one thing that made it worth living.'

The bitter-sweetness of it all tore at Keira's heart. Would it be so very wrong to allow herself the joy of playing make-believe for a few precious minutes before she told him the truth and had to watch him recoil from her? Why not? She had nothing left to lose, after all.

'If you're trying to tell me you love me...' she suggested, with great daring.

'Yes?'

'It might be easier to convince me if you showed me instead.'

It was just a game, just make-believe. And that was the reason, the only reason, she was able to make such a provocative appeal.

'Like this, you mean?'

He had crossed the room in a few strides to take her in his arms.

'You'll never know how much I've missed you,' he told her emotionally, before he kissed her.

This was heaven and hell all rolled into one—

pleasure and pain, joy and guilt—and she could not bear to relinquish either Jay or her make-believe dream that somehow there could be a happy-ever-after for them. But she knew that she must. She could not live a lie. She could not and would not deceive him a second time.

'I love you, Keira. I never thought I'd ever want to say those words to any woman, but now not only do I want to say them to you, I want to go on saying them, and not just saying them but living them. I want to hear you saying them to me. Is there any chance that you might do that, do you think?'

'I do love you Jay.' It was the truth, after all.

His kiss was so sweet and tender, so loving and giving— so very precious when she knew it could be their last.

'I recently opened a letter thanking me for my substantial gift. I take it that donating money to a charity that aids prostitutes was your way of underlining my offence, firstly in misjudging you and secondly in thinking I could buy you?'

It would be easy to be a coward and agree, but her conscience wouldn't let her. She took a deep breath and stepped out of the protection of his arms, fixing her gaze on the wall and not on Jay.

'Actually, I donated your money to that particular charity because of my mother. She was a prostitute, you see, and a drug addict.'

Silence.

'She's dead now. She died when I was twelve. Like mother, like daughter—that's what the great-aunt who took me in after her death used to say to me. It's what people think, isn't it? I feared at one stage that I could grow to be like her myself. She often said to me herself that I would.'

Still silence.

'You're shocked, of course. And disgusted. People are—it's only natural. What kind of responsible parent would want their child playing with a child whose mother sold her body to buy drugs? Certainly the parents of the children I was at school with didn't, and who could blame them? And what kind of man would want to take the risk of having a relationship with a woman whose mother had sex with men for money? You won't want me now, Jay. I know that. You have a responsibility, after all, to your name and to your position.'

'Was that why you stayed a virgin? Because of your mother?'

His question surprised her into looking at him. The silver-grey gaze was filled with something that looked close to pity. Pity? Shouldn't he be regarding her with contempt?

'Yes.'

'Tell me about it.'

Keira wanted to refuse, but somehow she discovered that instead she was telling him how she had felt—the pain of her childhood with its conflicting and confusing feelings, the love for her mother that had sometimes been more like anger and sometimes filled with despair.

'Once I was old enough to understand, I hated what she did,' she told him. 'And sometimes I hated her too, for being what she was. As I grew up we would quarrel about it. During one of our quarrels I told her that I was ashamed of her, and that I would never let myself end up like her. I probably hurt her, although I couldn't see that at the time. She laughed at me and told me that I wouldn't have a choice. She said that

since I was her daughter I had inherited her pro-
miscuous nature and that sooner or later, as she
put it, some lad would come along and I'd open
my legs for him. She said it would be expected
of me, and that—like her—I'd love the wrong
kind of men for the wrong kind of reasons.'

Keira had to stop talking to swallow against
her own sadness. Her mother must have felt so
alone and unloved, but she had never seen that
before. She had been too young and too emotionally immature herself then to see it. If
nothing else, loving Jay had taught her to view
her mother in a different and surely a fairer
light.

'What she said left me feeling both frightened
and angry. I swore to myself that if I had her
nature then I would make sure I controlled it.'

'By never having sex?' Jay guessed.

Keira nodded her head.

'Yes. It was easy until I met you. I never
guessed…I had no idea…'

'I made you feel that you were like your
mother?'

Keira shook her head.

'At first, yes. But then later, once we were lovers, my physical hunger for you showed me that I could never be like my mother. I wanted you so passionately, so exclusively, that I knew I could never give, never mind sell to another man, what I only wanted to give to you. I thank you for that, Jay—because knowing that has freed me from my fear of my own sexuality. My great-aunt and my mother both warned me that I would end up like my mother, but I know now that that will never happen. You won't want me now, of course.'

'On the contrary. If anything, what you have just told me makes me love you even more.'

Keira couldn't believe her ears.

'You can't love me now. I'm not good enough for you, Jay.'

'I am the one who isn't good enough for you. You are worth a hundred—no, a thousand of me, Keira. You humble me with your honesty and your compassion, your generosity of spirit and heart and your loyalty. I am not good enough for you, but that will not prevent me from having the arrogance to beg you to be my wife.'

'Your *wife?*'

'Of course.' Now the look he was giving her was indeed haughty.

'Do you think I would shame our love by not proclaiming it to the world in the most potent way the world recognises? And besides…' both his voice and his expression softened '…I refuse to let there be any chance of me losing you. Once you have committed yourself to me you will stay with me, and with our children. I know you well enough for that. You will be like my mother—faithful and loving. She would have liked you.'

'Jay, you cannot marry me. Your brother won't allow it. You are his heir.'

'Rao is my brother, not my keeper. I make my own decisions about my life. I have already told him of my desire to make you my wife, and he said that he had every sympathy for you.'

He laughed ruefully, and then shook his head.

'I do understand why you have thought the way you have. You have had much to bear and endure that I wish I could have spared you. But our happiness together will be all the sweeter because of the past pain we have both endured. I promise you that there is not a single thought or doubt in my heart or my head about the strength of my love for you. I promise you too that if you refuse me now I shall pursue you and plead with you until you give in and agree to marry me.'

Keira searched his expression, her heart lifting with joy when she saw that he was speaking the truth.

A little unsteadily, but with a heart filled with love, she went into his arms, lifting her face for his kiss.

EPILOGUE

KEIRA watched the busy preparations for the wedding ceremony from the shadows in the garden beyond the courtyard.

The sun was going down, and on the stillness of the lake the palace seemed to float as ethereally and delicately as the lilies.

In the courtyard the Mandap was being assembled; those wedding guests who had already arrived for tomorrow's ceremony were pausing to watch.

Keira saw the man emerging from the shadows to watch her. He was as male and formidable as the desert lion, and her heart lifted and thudded into her ribs, her breath catching on a swift stab of desire.

'Jay.'

'I thought I might find you here.'

They had been married in a civil ceremony in London earlier in the week, before flying back here to Jay's home to celebrate their marriage with a traditional marriage ceremony.

Last night Rao had held a formal dinner to welcome her into the family, but this was the first time she and Jay had really been alone since their arrival.

'You're wearing the bracelets,' Jay commented as he drew Keira into his arms.

'I couldn't resist,' Keira admitted.

He had given her the Cartier bangles on their first night together, after they had declared their love for one another in a very private celebration.

'What *I* can't resist is loving you,' Jay told her softly. 'Now and for ever.'

'Now and for ever,' Keira agreed, before she reached up to draw him down to her so that she could kiss him.

MILLS & BOON PUBLISH EIGHT LARGE PRINT TITLES A MONTH. THESE ARE THE EIGHT TITLES FOR FEBRUARY 2009.

 C₂

VIRGIN FOR THE BILLIONAIRE'S TAKING
Penny Jordan

PURCHASED: HIS PERFECT WIFE
Helen Bianchin

THE VÁSQUEZ MISTRESS
Sarah Morgan

AT THE SHEIKH'S BIDDING
Chantelle Shaw

BRIDE AT BRIAR'S RIDGE
Margaret Way

LAST-MINUTE PROPOSAL
Jessica Hart

THE SINGLE MUM AND THE TYCOON
Caroline Anderson

FOUND: HIS ROYAL BABY
Raye Morgan

MILLS & BOON®
Pure reading pleasure™

MILLS & BOON PUBLISH EIGHT LARGE PRINT TITLES A MONTH. THESE ARE THE EIGHT TITLES FOR MARCH 2009.

—————————— ∞ ——————————

RUTHLESSLY BEDDED BY THE ITALIAN BILLIONAIRE
Emma Darcy

MENDEZ'S MISTRESS
Anne Mather

RAFAEL'S SUITABLE BRIDE
Cathy Williams

DESERT PRINCE, DEFIANT VIRGIN
Kim Lawrence

WEDDED IN A WHIRLWIND
Liz Fielding

BLIND DATE WITH THE BOSS
Barbara Hannay

THE TYCOON'S CHRISTMAS PROPOSAL
Jackie Braun

CHRISTMAS WISHES, MISTLETOE KISSES
Fiona Harper

MILLS & BOON

Pure reading pleasure